# PISTOLS OR FISTS?

Bothwell shrugged and reached out to cut the wire.

"Don't do that," Lacy said, and Bothwell stopped, the cutters resting on the fence.

He turned to face Lacy. "How'd it be if I just whipped your ass for you, and no gun-play at all?"

Lacy thought about that. God knows he didn't want a shooting. On the other hand, this redhead looked like a handy fighter. And young. A beating or a shooting. He had stuck his nose in, and likely was about to get it bit off, one way or another. "I'll take a fist-fight, if I have to."

"Good for you," Bothwell said. "There's got to be more to you than there looks."

"Bud," Lacy said to the kid, "pull that Sharps. And either way it comes out, if that fat man touches his pistol, shoot him." He doubted the boy could beat the fat man to the draw, but it would be a way of seeing if the men were serious about this fist-fighting business.

"You ready for your whippin', Walkin' Fool?" Bothwell had his hands up like a boxer, showing off, smiling.

Lacy reached out for him and caught his shirt in both hands. He yanked Bothwell in and butted him in the face. Lacy hit out fast, then stepped in closer and kicked him in the groin.

He caught him good. It sounded like a horse-kick.

## Also in the BUCKSKIN Series:

# BUCKSKIN #3

---

# PISTOLTOWN

**Roy Le Beau**

LEISURE BOOKS ∞ NEW YORK CITY

A LEISURE BOOK

Published by

Dorchester Publishing Co., Inc.
6 East 39th Street
New York, NY 10016

Printed in the United States of America

*To the East side gang. . .*

# CHAPTER ONE

Bud Manugian was riding way up around the northeast hook of Angle Iron. A long day out from headquarters, a ten-hour day out, looking for wire breaks or wires down. If the break was bad enough, or it was posts busted, then the wagon crew would have to come out; Buddy was just a mender for small breaks. He was riding at the end of his day, squinting into the sunset, already looking for a brush patch or a ditch to slide off and unsaddle and roost in, to boil up the old coffee grounds the cookie had given him a handful of, and then mash his cold biscuits into the tin cup with the coffee. Angle Iron fed its hands well enough at headquarters, but cookie didn't waste fried meat on an A-rab kid doing a day's ride to mend fence.

Then Bud saw a man, instead of his brush patch or ditch. A man walking.

Bud looked down at his rifle, jammed deep in its boot beside the saddle horn. Not his rifle, really; it was a ranch gun, something they let the cowpushers check out of the kitchen shed if they were riding off alone, and didn't have one of their own. This rifle wasn't very good; it was an old

Henry with a weak trigger spring. You had to push the trigger forward, even after you'd levered the piece, to set it to fire. It was a pretty worn-out rifle. Bud had been saving for a hand-gun, but he only had seven dollars saved, and that wasn't near enough.

The man was walking along the outside of the fence. Walking south. Probably going to try and follow the fence all the way to the main buildings. That was a long way.

As he got closer to him, Bud saw that the walking man was carrying a saddle and bedroll and booted rifle on his back. He was walking slow and tired, too, pushing through the yellow chest-high panhandle grass, lugging that heavy saddle and bedroll. And the rifle.

Bud wondered again if he ought to pull the old Henry out, in case of trouble. Here was a man afoot; might be he'd like to take Blacky for himself, might put that rifle he was carrying on Bud—and just take little Blacky right out from under him.

Bud leaned over to tug at the Henry's stock—and saw that the man had stopped walking, and was standing still, watching him. Bud didn't know if he was embarrassed or just scared with the man looking at him like that, but he let go of the Henry's stock anyway, and sat up straight and looked back at the man so he wouldn't think he was scared of him. He knew he was already doing wrong, though. Mister Meager would have already had the walking man covered, and be riding right over to him to brace him good, just for being near Angle Iron fence. And the fellow would have to speak up pretty brisk to save himself a whipping. Would have to have a hurt horse for sure, and a good straight story to go with it, or look out. . .

The man was just standing in the high grass, looking at Bud. Then, after a while, he bent over and put the saddle down in the grass, and the booted rifle with it. Then he straightened up again, and stood watching Buddy the way he had before.

When Bud sat on his pony and didn't do anything, the man took off his hat and waved him in. It would have been too embarrassing not to do anything then, so Bud kicked Blacky up a little and rode over to the man at a slow walk.

"Come on," the man called to him. "I'm no horse thief."

When he got close to him, Bud saw that it didn't make any difference that the man had put his rifle down with his saddle. Through the grass stems, he could see the man was wearing a belt gun, a revolver with an odd angled grip to it.

"Seen a Bisley Colt before?" the man said to him, smiling up at him in a friendly enough way.

"I've heard of 'em, I guess." No use to be taken for a fool.

The man didn't say anything more after that, and Bud took a look at him. He was a tall man, and leaned-down, and he had whisker stubble on his face and a bad scar cutting across his left cheek. It made his mouth look funny, just underneath the scar. The corner of his mouth turned down on that side, like a man's who's just made some droll joke. He had dark gray eyes, the same dark slate color as his beat-out Stetson. The rest of his clothes were pretty raggedy, a saddle-tramp's fixin's for sure, and he was wearing an old buckskin vest with long fringes, black and greasy from skinning-grease and campfires.

A saddle-tramp for sure. Bud knew what Mister Meager would have said to this fellow. "Walk away from this fence, Mister, walk east or walk north, but walk away from this fence."

"Now, listen," Bud said.

The man didn't seem to pay him any mind. "Get down off that pony, boy," he said, "and see if you can find us some dry brush for a fire. You got anything to eat in those saddle-bags?''

"Biscuits," Bud said. "But—"

"Well, get down and dig 'em out, then." He looked up at Bud and smiled at him. He looked friendly enough when he smiled, except that his mouth was crooked under that scar.

"Coffee?" he said.

"Some, I suppose. . ."

"You suppose?" The man laughed. "Then climb down and start cooking some of that 'suppose.' "

Bud guessed there was nothing much else to do. It was all wrong, though; that was for sure. Mister Meager would be mad as hell.

He swung down off the black pony and started digging in his saddle-bags for the biscuits and coffee, and his frying pan.

"What's your name, boy?" the man said to him.

"Michael Manugian."

"Yeah? What do they call you?"

"They call me Bud. What's your name, Mister?"

"My name's. . .Finn. . . Finn Lacy."

Bud put the biscuits down on the grass. They were tied in his second-best kerchief. It was a bright red one, or had been, when it was new. It was all faded out, now. Then he put the frying pan and the coffee in its screw of brown butcher's paper down in the grass too.

"I guess I'll go get the kindling," he said.

"You go on. I'll unsaddle your horse."

Bud was well down the fence line, grubbing around in the brush like some dumb plow-jockey looking for branches of greasewood and sage he could break off, when he suddenly realized what a fool he had made of himself. All that damn drifter had to do was climb on old Blacky and ride right off.

Bud straightened up with a shout and jumped up out of the greasewood staring goggle-eyed back where the drifter had his horse. He jumped out of there like a jackrabbit, and he looked something like a jackrabbit, too.

The drifter was standing beside Blacky, looking at Bud and laughing at him. But the saddle was off. He'd taken the pony's saddle and bridle and stacked them in the grass beside the worn Brazos double-rig he'd been carrying on his back.

"Go on. Bring in that firewood!" he called out to Buddy. "I'm not stealing your horse!"

By dark, they had the coffee boiled and the biscuits scorched hot, and they both were putting the grub away like lobo wolves. There wasn't much of it.

"I haven't seen hide nor hair of as much as a rabbit," the drifter said, "for a day and a half." He dipped a piece of biscuit into the steaming coffee. Buddy had forgotten his cup—he'd used it for his weekly shave, and then left it out in back of the bunkhouse by the pump when he'd packed up to ride—so they were both dipping out of the frying pan.

"Well," Bud said, "there's usually a lot of game out here, but the Comanche have been going through the last few weeks, doing their spring hunting, I guess."

The drifter looked up pretty sharp at that. "I thought those people were whipped. I thought Colonel Mackenzie put them down for good."

"Well, I guess he did. I heard he did, too. And I don't think they kill people around here the way they used to—but they're sure around. You don't see them very much, except out on the Stake Plains. You see them out there, sometimes. I saw some once, out there."

11

"And they still do a big spring hunt, huh?"

"They sure do, up here, anyway. They ride out of the Stake Plains."

"*Staked* Plains."

"Well, that's what I said. They ride out of there and they hunt anything they like."

The drifter shook his head. "If I'd known that, Bud, I sure wouldn't have been doing my walking in the daytime."

"Well, I haven't heard that they killed anybody lately."

"Be just my luck to change theirs," the drifter said, and he laughed.

They finished the biscuits and coffee, and sat for awhile looking at the little fire. The drifter—what was his name? —Lacy. Finn Lacy. He didn't look so hard now, in the firelight. Bud could see wrinkles on his face, and there was gray in his hair; you could see it over his ears when he tilted the Stetson brim up. He was practically an old man, really. The scar on his left cheek looked red in the firelight. That must have been a bad accident, Bud thought. Or somebody cut him there with a knife.

He was quick, though. He caught onto some of what Buddy had been thinking.

"How old are you, boy?"

Bud thought about lying, giving himself another year. He did that sometimes; he'd tried it when he'd first come to Angle Iron. But this fellow was pretty sharp, for all that he was just a tramp with no horse, and he looked like he'd laugh if he caught Buddy out. "Fifteen—and more than a half."

"Well now," the drifter said, "I guess that's old enough to hold down a man's job."

"It damn sure is," Bud said, just so this Lacy wouldn't have any doubts about it. "You bet."

He could ask questions too. "What happened to your horse, Mister Lacy?"

"Dead," the drifter said. "Tired out and got old and fell down, and died." He gave Bud a look across the fire. "Just like I will—and just like you will, too."

Nothing much Bud could say to that. This fellow was likely half crazy as not. Most of these circuit saddle-bums were; that's what Mister Meager said, and the men said, too.

"You're an Armenian, are you?" the drifter said to him after a while.

"Like hell I am! I'm an American, Mister!" And if this old son-of-a-bitch didn't like that, then he could just lump it!

"No offense," the drifter said, and he stretched out in the grass, propped his head up in his hand and looked into the fire.

Neither of them said anything for a while.

The drifter sat up and put a bundle of sage-branches on the fire to keep it up. "Probably bring those damn Comanches down on us," he said. "So, what do your bunkies call you—'Jewboy' or 'A-rab'?"

Bud didn't say anything for a while, then he said, "A-rab."

Lacy laughed. "And you no such thing." He threw another branch on the fire. "The hell with the Comanches. I knew an Armenian in San Francisco some time ago. You ever hear of a man called Ara Kerkorian?"

"No, I never did."

"He was a gambler. Good dealer, too. He dealt blackjack down on the Coast."

"I'm going to go to San Francisco one day," Bud said. "When I do, maybe I'll look that fellow up."

Lacy lay back down in the grass, tilting the brim of his

Stetson down over his eyes to shade them from the firelight. "How come you got to cowpunching, Bud?"

Bud thought maybe he ought to tell this man that that was his own personal business, then he thought that if he did, Lacy would just laugh at him.

"Well. . . my mother got sick and died."

"That so?"

"Well, she died. . . and my daddy'd died before that, I guess. He was a peddler—hardware and software, you know. He went up into Oklahoma Territory a long time ago, and he didn't ever get back. We never heard what happened to him, or the wagon and team, neither."

"He must have had more guts than sense, then," Lacy said from under his Stetson. "To take trading goods up into the Territory in the old days."

Bud didn't know how to take that.

"My daddy was smart," he said.

Lacy didn't pay any attention to him. "More guts than sense to do a thing like that. Guess he was thinking of doing some good trading up there. Was some money to be made in the Territory—if a man could stay alive."

Bud didn't say anything for a while, then he said, "Well. . . what do you know about it?"

"More than enough," the drifter said, and yawned. "Now, we better put a lid on it, boy. Morning'll be coming on pretty quick. And if we don't run across a rabbit, I'm liable to eat that pony of yours for breakfast. My belly button's kissing my backbone." He rolled half-over to tug his blanket from his bedroll, wrapped himself in it, and stretched out facing away from the fire.

Bud sat up at the fire some time after that, thinking, and enjoying being awake and ready for any kind of trouble at the fire, while this drifter who acted so wise and talked so big was worn out and sound asleep. He was lucky Bud didn't just fork old Blacky and ride out on him.

Then, Bud poured the last of the coffee over the fire, and stood up and stepped out what was still burning. He wasn't scared of Comanches. He guessed they'd know better than to fool with two armed white men. The drifter was probably pretty tough, and if it turned out he was all bluff, well, Bud thought he could probably show those Indians something. If he got a chance, he might just turn out to be a damn good hand with that old Henry. A damn good hand. . .

When the boy was asleep, Lacy got up, checked that the fire was full out. Then he took a little walk, to piss, see the pony hadn't stepped out of its hobbles, to look around in the moonlight, to find if any trouble might be riding their way. The Panhandle grass was white in the moonlight. It lay rolling out to the horizon all about him, white as snow. White as snow in the mountains to the north.

The gentle night wind stirred the grass. Lacy heard the grass stems hissing softly as the wind combed through them. It sounded like the snow blowing, drifting, in the Bitterroot mountains.

Bud was a good enough kid. Lacy had seen plenty of the worked-down, snot-nose, and kiss-my-ass-and-draw-your-gun pup that came running out to Texas ranches to play the game of cowboy. Most of them weren't worth much, and got to be worth less as the older hands bullied them or spoiled them—or just plain worked them silly. But Bud seemed to be a nice enough kid. His mother had time enough to raise him gentle before she died. A lot of ranch boys had been raised up like stray dogs, and showed it.

Maybe too nice, too gentle for the life; small and

15

skinny—looked more like fourteen than sixteen with that big nose sticking out and eyes like a just-dropped calf's.

The boy was up on his pony now—Angle Iron's pony, really, since that was the outfit the boy'd said he worked for. The boy was up, though when they'd rolled out of their suggins at dawn it appeared he still thought Lacy was going to do him dirt and steal the horse and ride off laughing.

The boy was up, with Lacy's saddle and bedroll tied in a heap behind him. It wasn't tidy, but it was the best that could be done—the little black horse sure couldn't carry double for far. Lacy would walk a while, then the kid would walk a while, though he didn't seem too pleased with that part of the arrangement.

Lacy had slid the boy's old Henry—Angle Iron's old Henry, probably—up out of the boot, and carried it over his shoulder as he walked along. Little Bud had looked real grim when Lacy'd done that, so Lacy had handed him the big Sharps up to put in its place. Having that cannon beside him as he rode seemed to settle Bud down just fine.

Lacy was looking for a jackrabbit. It was spring, and too early for the worms to have ruined the meat. A big jack would cook up fine, and the Henry was the rifle for that; a slug from the Sharps would leave no breakfast at all.

North Texas here was fine looking country, if you liked grass. High grass, and rolling land, and square miles, and sections, and counties. Not a tree in a hundred miles, north, east, south or west. Country, and hot sun.

# CHAPTER TWO

It was a chore, being afoot on this rough ground, wading through the chest-high grass. But a damn sight easier than it had been when he was lugging that saddle and bedroll. He'd give the boy an hour up, and then do some riding himself.

They were working along the three-strand fence, still heading north. The boy'd had another short side section to do before turning back to the ranch, and Lacy'd seen no reason to force him off his work. It would mean a couple more miles walking, but hell, his boots were busted down already—couldn't do much more harm.

He saw the boy, riding ahead a little, pull the black pony up and swing down out of the saddle, the brim of his ragged, brown wool hat flopping as he hit the ground with the wire-tool in his hand. Lacy could see the top strand of barb wire sagging off the post there, and Bud was hauling it back up into place, and digging a staple out of the pocket of his canvas jacket to fasten it back up. He got the wire up, the staple over it, and hammered it fast with four hard strokes of the narrow tool-head. Kid did his job.

"Wire seems in fair shape," Lacy said.

"It is, when they leave it alone."

"Say what?"

But the boy climbed back onto his pony and kicked it into a walk and didn't say anything more.

Lacy walked on after him, feeling the morning sun already hot on his shoulders.

No jackrabbits; no antelope either, though these Texas plains were home to the critters. There were still buffalo down here, but not a sight of living hide or hair. Damn all. He heard his stomach growl with hunger.

Lacy saw a small flock of birds fly up from a patch of brush on a shallow rise ahead. Small birds, songbirds, likely. And where were the damn prairie hens? The Comanches couldn't have taken all the game in the country.

Up ahead, he saw the boy pull the pony in again. Must be more slack wire. . .

Two horsemen rode out of the brush at an easy canter, and came down toward them.

Lacy walked up alongside the boy. "Some pards of yours, I guess," he said.

"No," the boy said. "No, they're not."

The horsemen were a stone's-throw away.

"What did you say?" Lacy said to the boy. And he eased the keeper-loop off the hammer of his holstered Colt.

"I said they're. . . no friends of mine." Bud's voice was pitched higher than it had been. Lacy saw the boy's hand trembling as he reached over to tug at the butt of the booted Sharps.

"Take your hand away." Lacy said to him. "Don't touch that piece."

"Well, now, hey there!" The first rider called to them, pulling his big pinto down to a walk, breasting the horse through the high grass.

Lacy walked around in front of the boy's pony, into a patch of shorter grass by the fence.

"Now, look-a here!" the horseman said. "Look-a here, Louis. We got a fella prefers walking to ridin' horses!" He laughed.

The horseman was a handsome young man in his early twenties. He had bright blue eyes and his nose had been broken. He had pale, freckled skin, and a lantern jaw.

"Good morning to you, Dad," he said, and took his flat-crown Montana hat off and bowed to Lacy from the saddle. He had curly, carrot-red hair. He smiled and winked. "Dad, you look all walked out." The big pinto sidled, sweating from its run.

Lacy didn't say anything.

The other rider sat still on a chunky roan, looking at Lacy. He was a fat man, in his thirties, with a dark-red spade beard. He looked sleepy, bored. He had a parrot-grip .38 stuck in his belt.

"Now, what do you say to this, Louis? Here's little A-rab and he's got a walkin' fool checkin' fence with him. What do you say to that?"

"Stop your foolin', Abe," the fat man said.

The young man paid him no mind. He smiled at Lacy from atop the big pinto. "You will allow me to introduce myself," he said. "Abraham Bothwell, at your service. And this here fine figure of a man is my brother, Louis."

"Howdy." Lacy said.

"Why you walkin' son-of-a-bitch," Bothwell said, "how you do chatter at a man!" He turned back in his saddle to wink at his brother. "You ever hear of such a loudmouth, Louis?"

"Get along on with it," his brother said.

"Yep," Abe Bothwell said. "That's enough socializin'. Time for us folks to get down to business!" He swung lightly out of the saddle and stepped down into the grass. Then he took a wire cutter from his back pocket and walked over to the fence. The pinto was a good horse; it stood still where he'd left it.

"Don't you touch that wire!"

Lacy glanced around, and saw that Bud Manugian was reaching for the butt of the Sharps.

"If you *touch* that rifle, Little Bit, I'm goin' to kill you cold." The red-headed man was standing beside the fence with the wire cutters in his hand, smiling at the boy. He didn't seem angry. He was wearing two Remington .44's, butts forward for cross draws. His hands were nowhere near them.

"You see what a beautiful spring day this here's goin' to be, A-rab? You wouldn't want to miss the rest of this day, now, would you, boy?" He glanced at Lacy, and winked at him. "Why you'd be missin' the rest of your whole life!"

"Come on, get it cut," said the fat man sitting on the roan.

"Don't you touch that wire!" The boy's voice broke at the end.

"Didn't anybody hear a mouse around here?" Bothwell said, laughing, and he turned to cut the wire.

"Leave it alone," Lacy said. And it cost him to say it to stick his nose in. But how the hell could he not?

Bothwell, reaching for the wire with the cutters, stopped still. He turned his head and looked at Lacy, smiling. "I can see," he said, "that you don't know the lay of the land, not in this part of Texas."

"Tell me about it," Lacy said. "But don't touch that wire."

Bothwell called out to his brother. "What do you think, Louis? Do you think we'd be wise to kill the both of 'em?"

The fat man thought about it.

"It's a lot of killin'. Not supposed to be that much trouble, yet."

"Now, Louis, you have a point there." He smiled at Lacy, and said, "You see how it is, I guess." He shook his head. "I suppose older brothers are the same all over. 'Do this, don't do that.'" He raised his voice. "Now, Louis, if we don't kill these two poor fellas, then what the deuce do we do with 'em?"

His brother sat on the roan, thinking.

Bothwell winked. "While old Louis is figurin' it out, Mister Walkin' Fool, let me advise you that the Central Cattle Company has a right-of-way agreement through this section. You know what right-of-way is, Dad?"

Lacy nodded.

Bothwell shook his head. "There you are, jabberin' away again!" He laughed. "But you do understan' me, don't you? We got the *law* on our side."

"You're a liar!" Bud had put in his two cents.

Bothwell looked up at him in a friendly way. "I sure am, Little A-rab. No doubt about that. But the law's the law."

"Abe," the fat man said.

"Yep?"

"We're not supposed to have so much trouble as killin' both of them."

Bothwell shrugged. "There you are," he said to Lacy, and reached to cut the wire.

"Don't do that," Lacy said, and Bothwell stopped, the cutters resting on the fence.

"Mister—" The fat man shifted on his roan.

"No, Louis—I think I got the answer to our problem." He turned to face Lacy. "How'd it be, Dad, if I just whipped your ass for you, and no gun-play at all?"

Lacy thought about that. God knows he didn't want a shooting. He was too damn tired to run from a shooting.

On the other hand, this redhead looked a handy fighter. And young.

A beating—or a shooting. He had stuck his nose in, and likely was about to get it bit off, one way or another.

"I'd rather have breakfast," he said, "but I'll take a fist-fight, if I have to."

"Good for you," Bothwell said. "There's got to be more to you than there looks."

"Bud," Lacy said, "pull that Sharps. And either way it comes out, if that fat man touches his pistol, shoot him." It wasn't much, and Lacy doubted the boy could beat the fat man, Louis, to the shoot—but it would be a way of seeing if the men were serious about this fist-fight business.

It seemed they were. They glanced at each other, but neither made a move to their guns while Bud hauled the big rifle out of the boot and drew the hammer full back.

"Let's get to it," Bothwell said; he seemed to Lacy to be looking forward to it. He unbuckled his crossed gunbelts and draped them over the fence wire. Then he made a funny face at Lacy, reached behind his back and came out with a broad-bladed Bowie knife. He stuck the knife into the top of the fence post, stepped aside, took off his hat and rolled up his sleeves.

Lacy shed his Colt, and his hat, bent and slid the Arkansas toothpick out of his right boot, and put them both out of the way, under the bottom fence wire. He'd have to watch out for the fence—it would be no pleasure to fall against those barbs.

"You ready for your whippin', Walkin' Fool?" Bothwell had his hands up like a boxer. He did a quick little dance in the grass, showing off, smiling. He was light on his feet.

"Come on, Abe," his brother said.

Bothwell danced in, hit Lacy backhand across the eyes with his left hand and punched him in the throat with his right. He was very quick.

22

He came in again, and Lacy swung at him, slowly.

"Oh-oh, you're in trouble, Walkin' Fool."

He came in, hit Lacy in the temple and then on the side of the neck. Lacy was knocked into the fence and his arm hooked on the wire-barbs for a moment. He pulled free and swung at Bothwell again. Another slow swing.

"Meat on the table," the red-head said. He came in again, hitting hard.

Lacy reached out for him—fast, this time—and caught his shirt in both hands. He yanked Bothwell in, and butted him in the face. He felt the man's nose break, and then shoved him away hard. Bothwell pedaled back, blowing the blood out of his nose. Lacy hit out fast at his face, pulled the punch when the man got his hands up high, then stepped in closer and kicked him in the nuts.

He caught him good. It sounded like a horse-kick.

Bothwell was a hard case. He stayed standing up straight for a few moments, and he kept his hands up, too. But Lacy saw the blind look in his eyes—no smiling or winking, now—and knew he was hurt bad.

Then, Bothwell began to bend. Slowly, slowly, he began to stoop over, bending at the waist, his hands coming down. Lacy stepped back, closer to where he'd put the Colt down, and glanced over at the older brother. But Louis Bothwell was doing nothing. His sat on his chunky roan like a side of bacon, looking at Lacy without much interest.

"You beat him! You beat him!" Buddy Manugian was bouncing in his saddle, the cocked Sharps waving this way and that.

"Watch that rifle, boy."

Abe Bothwell was trying to catch his breath. He went down on one knee, still doubled over, gasping, trying to hold his head up.

Lacy got his Colt and holstered it, slid the toothpick back into his boot.

"You beat him!" Buddy was a happy A-rab.

Louis Bothwell hadn't said anything. He didn't seem angry. He didn't seem very interested.

The three of them watched Abe. And he was a hard case. He pulled in a long, ragged breath, got his feet under him, and slowly stood up. It took a while. And he couldn't stand straight.

"Now," he said to Lacy, and his voice sounded pretty good, "now, I guess I played prime jackass to you, drifter." He tried a smile, and it came off well enough. "I should a' seen you was too slow to be true."

He walked over to the fence for his guns, and he walked straight, but it cost him.

"Now," he said, buckling the guns on, "I'm sure as hell goin' to kill you soon as we get the go-ahead, you scar-face son-of-a-bitch." He tried a smile. "But I'm damn sure not drawin' against anybody today. Feels like I'd lose everything I got did I move too quick." He pulled his knife out of the fence post.

"Next time, though," He bent down with a grunt to pick up the wire cutters. "Next time, though, I'll sure put you under." He bent down again for his hat.

"Come on, Abe," Louis Bothwell said.

Abe climbed onto his big pinto, but didn't sit in the saddle. He stood in the stirrups.

His brother turned his roan and kicked it into a trot; when the pinto moved out to follow, Lacy heard Abe say, "Jumpin' Jesus Christ!" under his breath. It must have hurt considerable."

Lacy stood and watched them out of sight. It took a while. Louis rode straight away, and didn't slow for his brother at all. Abe followed along behind, keeping up off

24

the saddle as well as he could. In a few minutes they had ridden into the brush on the rise, and out of sight.

"You beat up Abe Bothwell. . ." Buddy still had the Sharps clutched in his hands.

"Ease the hammer on that rifle, boy, and put the damn thing away." Lacy watched the rise a while longer, making sure the Bothwells had no second thoughts about being run off that way. He was not so impressed by the Bothwells as he was by whoever gave them their orders. Most gunmen would have put him and the boy down fast—or at least tried to—the moment it even looked to be gun trouble. The Central Cattle Company must be a hard-nose outfit, and hungry—the Bothwells were a long cut above the average hard case cowpushers most outfits used in range trouble.

Range trouble. The oldest trouble there was—and worse now, with the range closing down.

Trouble he didn't intend to have any part of.

Despite the Bothwells—and this damn fence-line scramble just now.

# CHAPTER THREE

"Mister Lacy. . ." He turned and saw the boy climbing down off the black pony. "You ride him now."

Lacy wasn't about to say "no." His head was hurting something fierce where Bothwell had hit him, and his throat hurt too. Getting a little bit too old for these fisticuffs, is what it amounted to. Bothwell had been fast, and strong—and young. If he hadn't fallen for Lacy being such a slowpoke with a punch, it would have ended the other way, and Lacy knew it.

Lacy swung up on the pony, and led out at a walk, Bud Manugian scuffing along beside him, the old Henry over his shoulder. Lacy saw that the boy was imitating him, the way he walked and carried the rifle. It didn't please him.

The pony must have been the tail end of the Angle Iron string, the wranglers shucking him off on the boy, because the little horse had the roughest walk Lacy'd ever felt. He sort of stumped along as if his legs weren't bending. Felt like he had three legs—or maybe five.

Lacy was damn glad he wasn't running him. Just the walk alone was making his head-ache worse.

He considered the Bothwells as gun-hands, not that he intended to stay in north Texas long enough to see them working. Abe now, the young one, was likely just as fast with the Remingtons as with his fists. Probably took a smooth long circle across his belly for the cross-draw, like most of the Texicans. Old fashioned. But quick enough, if you're young enough.

That fat Louis was a horse of a different color—nothing very quick about him. More likely he sat quiet while his brother made the noise. Then, when he'd made up his mind, he'd just take his pistol out and shoot you with it. No stand-up-and-damn-your-eyes about it. They'd make a good pair. With young Abe doing so much talking, it was a little hard to keep your mind on Louis as well. To remember that he was sitting there, quiet, making up his mind.

The Bothwells were likely all right. A good cut above the usual, for sure. Lacy doubted they'd keep a mad concerning the boy. He was the one they'd remember. Abe would remember him for sure. Well let them. He'd be long gone as fast as he could go. He had the money for a horse—maybe not enough for a very good horse, and then it would be down to the border. Down to the border and back to Mexico. *Mexico.* After three years. A little more than three years. The Don would give him work down there. . .the old thief. But first, a horse. He'd never find one as good all round, sprint and long-travel, as that good old dun.

"Bud," he said, "how much more wire have you got to check before we can ride down to your headquarters?"

"Across there is the last stretch, Mister Lacy." Marching along with the Henry over his shoulder. And probably couldn't hit a barrel from the inside with the piece.

"Lacy."

"Sir?"

"Skip the 'Mister,' just call me 'Lacy.' "

"Yes, sir."

"And skip the 'sir,' too."

"Yes. . .Lacy."

Lacy didn't know if his head was hurting worse from hunger, or Bothwell's punches.

"I'll watch the fence, Bud," he said. "You look out for something to shoot. My belly thinks my throat's cut."

"Okay. Happy to do it."

Nothing like kicking a man in the nuts to get a nice boy's admiration. Lacy'd had that admiration before. Had liked it very well upon a time.

*Look-a there! I told yuh he just wears the one gun! A Bisley Colt's with a plain walnut handle. . . Look-a there!* They used to come around like flies, little kids on up to grown men, peering into the barrel-house windows, pushing their noses against the glass. . .

And there was the big man—a pretty *young* big man, at that—lying back at ease, tilting back in a busted straw-seat chair, with the butt of that Bisley sticking out like his dingus, and a glass of beer in his hand. A mighty fierce fellow. A damn rough cob. And a sport, to boot. Dressed up like a Boston gent—well, a San Francisco gent. Fine whipcord pants, a shirt made of Chinese silk. Soft Mexican boots. The best. And the buckskin vest. So people would know who they were dealing with.

Trouble. A fine young killer. A class mack. A prime cadet. Break in a girl—or break a man. All one to that handsome devil. . .

"You're the prettiest cow-flop I've seen," Holliday had said. "The genuine article."

Strange that he and Holliday had never quarreled. Not seriously. They'd liked each other; there didn't seem room enough for a bad quarrel between them. And they weren't afraid of each other. That was the most important thing.

They weren't afraid of each other—so they didn't have to fight.

The Lord knows he could have beaten Doc to the draw from a sound sleep and upside down. Doc wasn't quick at all, for a prime gun. He could beat an ordinary man to the draw for sure. But he wasn't really *quick*, not the way Hickok was, or Wes Hardin. Not as fast as Earp, for that matter.

"True, true," Doc used to say. "I'm no cottontail with a pistol." He'd roll those sad pop-eyes. "But Lord have mercy, do I kill 'em!"

That was true enough. Doc just killed 'em. And happy to do it with a straight-edge razor, if one was handy. . .

Gone now.

Long gone. And to no .45 or dagger, either. Drowned in blood in his bed. . .

"This is funny. . ."

The nurse at Denver, at the sanitarium, said that was what he said while he was dying.

"This here's the last stretch Mis—Lacy."

"Well, thank God for that! Let's head on in to that outfit you work for. Here, you ride this pony for a while. He's just too damn much horse for me to handle."

Walking was better than riding—at least better than riding that pony. His head felt better. Just a dull ache, now, and that might be just missing breakfast, and no food the day before. But Bothwell could hit, no doubt about that. There was still something of that sick feeling that comes when you've been hit hard.

No doubt though, that Abe Bothwell would be feeling worse. It would teach him to lean on a weary scarface drifter. Next time, he'd be watching for punches just a bit too clumsy, too slow to be the McCoy. . .

Lacy?''

"Yep?"

"I just wanted to tell you. . .that Henry's got kind of a bad trigger on it. You have to push it with your finger to get it to set right.''

"Right. Thanks for telling me, Bud. Now, if we can only see something to shoot, you can bet I'll get that trigger set just fine.''

The sun was up high now, coming on near to noon. It would be full dark for sure before they made it to the place. He could be grateful the dun hadn't dropped farther out. Most panhandle spreads ran about 40—50,000 acres. He could have damn well starved to death if he'd tried walking all the way in from the last line. Starved—or eaten the dun. He have run out of water, too, two-quart canteen or not. . .

The grass was blazing yellow under the sunlight. Hot. It was going to be a stinger, no doubt. Texas spring was Idaho summer. The sun was weighing on him already, dust and grasshoppers drifting up out of the high grass every step he took. He was wading through it, feeling last year's grass clumped, packed under his boots as he walked. Good cow country. . . or was until '86. Must've had to re-stock the entire range down here after that winter.

"Bud?''

The boy turned in the saddle to look down at him. A young one, for sure. Wouldn't be shaving for another two or three years. . .

"You people re-stocked this range, have you?'' Lacy got a sudden picture of a big steer pitched down by the old Henry. A good five-pound chunk cut out of the small of its back. A brush fire, sputtering fat and char-cooking beef. Hell, they couldn't hang a man for killing to eat! Not much, they couldn't.

"We re-stocked some, but Angle's a winter-feed spread.

Was during the big winter, too. Mister Meager says they did better than most.''

*Better than most.* And that was why that Cattle Company outfit was after the Angle Iron. No use rushing some boned-out outfit with burned-over grass and froze-hoof longhorns. Angle Iron was still fat, as Panhandle ranches went these days.

"Smart," Lacy said. "To winter-feed." Too smart for their own good. Go under or get took, was what it amounted to. Time for a smart fool to head for old Mexico, and double quick.

"It's the only way, Mister Meager says."

"Who's this Meager, Bud?"

"Mister Meager's the foreman," the boy said, in about the same tone preachers talk about Jesus Christ.

"Where's the stock?" Lacy said. "We haven't seen hide nor hair."

"We're finishing spring round up, is why; we got 'em bunched in the west section." He glanced down at Lacy from the pony. "If you was to think you'd want a job, Angle might be hirin' on just now."

"I don't think so, kid."

A ranch job. In a range war.

No thanks. Not interested in the work; not any more. No more working with the land, the stock. No more getting out into before-dawn dark, slapping your sides to keep warm while the chuck shack coffee started boiling on the stove. No more saddling up with cold-stiffened fingers, warming the bit under your arm so it won't burn the horse's mouth. No more looking out over your own range, your horses galloping down the mountain meadows, running through the dwarf willows along the Rifle river. . .

No thanks, boy, not interested in the work. Not any more.

And, sure as hell is hot, not interested in the killing that would go with it, down here.

Not any more.

It was the good men it hurt to remember. That fine, tough old border gunman in Montana. There was a hard old case. Had shot Lacy damn near to pieces, and already dying himself. You'd look a long way to find a better man than that old killer.

And Shannon. There was a fellow could have been a friend. You knew that, just meeting him, just looking him in the eyes.

Could have been. . .

Too many years of "could have beens." Too damn much to remember. Too damn many people to remember.

Lacy kicked his way through the high grass, feeling the sun-hot length of the Henry weighing across his shoulder. They'd come across only that one down-wire the whole morning. Angle Iron's fences were well kept up. Though why the hell this foreman, Meager, was sending a kid out to ride fence—even home section fence—alone, while there was range trouble cooking, was hard to figure.

A horse—and then Mexico. And food. He'd give considerable for a bowl of Chalusca chili beef right now. And a stack of foot-wide tortillas to scoop it with. If he didn't get *some* food in him before long, he was going to start staggering like a just-dropped calf. His head was hurting something fierce from hunger and Abe Bothwell combined. Beginning to wish the young son-of-a-bitch—all that damn winking and smiling—had decided to make it a shooting affair. Bothwell'd be stone dead by now, and likely cooked and eaten as well! Lacy'd had human meat once, or just the one time he knew about for sure, in a Cree camp on the North Fork, up in Canada. It was in a stew, with some dog meat and cooked greens. The Crees had told him what it was, grinning all over their faces, but he had thought they

32

were funning, the way Indians will do with a white man. He'd eaten all his portion just the same, and it had been good. Then, a while later, he'd gone tramping out of camp to shit in a snow bank in the birches, and damned if he hadn't seen a man's leg sticking up out of the snow right near there. It was a naked Indian leg with a dirty moccasin still on the foot. An Ojibway moccasin. The thing was frozen blue, and they'd cut the whole calf away between knee and ankle.

When he'd walked back to camp, Lacy'd kept a calm, straight face about it, as if he'd seen nothing out there. But the Crees knew. They all looked at him and smiled and smiled. He'd made their day amusing for them, up there on the North Fork. Nothing Indians liked better than making a fool out of a white man. Easy enough to do, at that. Still and all, that meat had tasted all right. The stew had tasted better than dog stew usually did. He remembered thinking that, even while he was eating it.

So Bothwell might be missing a slice off his rump, had it come to killing there by the fence. Lacy laughed out loud, thinking of Bud Manugian's face, if the boy had witnessed something like that.

He walked along through the high grass, laughing. And when the boy turned around in his saddle to see what Lacy was laughing about, he laughed even harder.

"What is it?" the boy called, smiling. He was a friendly boy.

"I was thinking that if only I'd killed that Bothwell back there, we could have fried him up and ate him!"

The boy sat back in his saddle and laughed. "Well, maybe just his liver." he called back. "Say, Lacy, you want to get up on old Blacky again?"

"No. I'm too hungry to get near that fat little horse of yours, Bud."

Bud grinned back at Lacy, and patted the pony's rump. "Not my Blacky," he said.

They were heading along the fence, up the slow, sweeping rise to a ragged line of greasewood to the south. It wasn't much of a high point, maybe thirty feet over the level of the prairie. Lacy saw some birds fly out of the greasewood, some small songbirds rising out of the brush in a bunch, turning, flying off west, skimming the tops of the grass. Lacy levered a round into the Henry's chamber, remembered the bad trigger, and eased it forward with his thumb until he felt it engage. A thing like that wrong with a weapon could get a man killed, should he be in a hurrying situation.

"Say Bud!"

"Yes sir?"

"See those birds fly out of there—on that rise?"

Lacy saw the boy look ahead, nod, and then reach the Sharps up out of its boot beside the saddle-bow, cock it, then cradle the piece in his arms as he rode.

Good boy. If the Bothwells *had* changed their minds after all, and came riding down all of a sudden, they'd collect some rifle lead before they hit the flats. Rifles. Lacy didn't much like them for fighting. Hunting was another thing. It had always seemed to him a coward's way. To mark a man down farther than you could make out his face. It wasn't really fighting at all. It was just butchering, win or lose.

He stopped a moment to get his breath; it was hot as a brickyard furnace standing in the grass. The bright green and yellow stems and grass-tops reflected the sunlight back up, shimmering under his hat-brim, glaring up in his eyes. The rim of the sky seemed more white than blue. And not even summer, yet.

Then, during the Panhandle summer, if a man were to be set afoot, and try to walk out of this country, well, that sun would fall on him like fire, and bake his brains. It would kill him sure.

In the heat haze, in among the green-gold tangles of the grass, Lacy saw quick small spots of bright blue, the first blue bonnets coming up, growing with the buffalo grass, the grama. Small dots of bright blue scattered through the green and yellow. In time, in a month or two, the prairie would be running with long bright drifts of blue, rivers of blue like spilled ink as the flowers bloomed among the grass. Then, for a short while, north Texas looked like heaven—if you didn't look too close.

He saw Bud Manugian suddenly pull his pony in, lifting the Sharps.

Two horsemen were standing on the rise, looking down at them. Dark small figures, wavering in heat haze. Then they turned their horses toward, and spurred them into a run, riding down at Lacy and the boy side by side. Running through the grass, the horses stepped high, as though they were pacing down through a sea of gold.

# CHAPTER FOUR

It wasn't the Bothwells.

No pinto. One man was riding a black, the other, a short-necked sorrel. Both cowpushers, by their style.

"Say, Pete!" Bud Manugian sang out. Friends, then—Angle Iron men. Lacy stood back, and kept the Henry over his shoulder, and watched the two ride up. The outboard one threw him a glance as they pulled up by the boy and his pony in a yellow fog of dust and buzzing grass-hoppers. The outboard man was small and sunburned black, with a big pointy-crown Stetson pulled near down to his ears. He had dark eyes and a go-get-'um look on his face. An old Confederate piece—maybe a Whitely—jammed down into the belt of his chaps.

The other rider was a plump fellow in a black and white check shirt and dirty wool pants. He had a face as red and round as a baby's, and popped blue eyes.

"Say, now, Bud," he said to Bud Manugian, "You supposed to have rid into headquarters this *mornin'*, not have left it for men to come out here to see ain't no jumpin' mouse carried you off!"

"Mister Lacy and me—"

"Say what?" the plump man said, and rolled his popped blue eyes down at Lacy. "Mister which?" His eyes were red-rimmed from the dust he'd been riding through. "I don't see no 'Mister' walking on Iron ground." He leaned side-ways in his saddle. Lacy saw a hard, round bulge of gut in the checked shirt. "Looks like a driftin' bum to me. You been walkin' this bum into the ranch, Bud?"

Lacy didn't say anything. He stood in the chest-high grass with the Henry across his shoulder, and gazed in a general way at the two cowboys. He saw that the little sunburned one didn't like listening to the plump one talk.

"He beat up Abe Bothwell, Pete! He kicked him right in the clams!"

The plump one gave Lacy another look. Lacy saw he had no hand-gun on him, but he carried a cut-down shotgun in a short leather bucket behind the cantle of his saddle.

"Do tell?"

The sunburned one let out a yip. "Did he?" he said. "Did he do that, now?" He had a strange accent, like an English accent or maybe Candian, but slower, with a sharp whine to it. Lacy had heard it before.

Nevada. Sheep people out there. . . Mister Riles. This cowpusher was an Australian.

"They went to it bare-handed," the boy was saying, building up it up big, "and Abe hit Lacy and tried to drag him on the fence—and it looked real close, *real* close—and then Lacy kicked old Abe Bothwell right in the clams! And that was all she wrote. Yes sir!"

"Do tell?" the plump man said.

"Is that the truth?" the sunburned man said to Lacy.

"Near enough," Lacy said.

"Well, good on you," the sunburned man said, and leaned down in his saddle and held out his hand to shake.

"Harry Pierce's my name."

"Lacy." The Australian had a wire-thin grip, very strong.

"All right, Lacy, you climb up behind on old Tiger here, and I'll give you a ride down to the ranch."

Lacy handed up the Henry, then reached up to grip the saddle cantle and hauled himself up behind Harry Pierce. The sorrel grunted and shifted under the extra weight.

"Quiet, Tiger," Pierce said, and thumped the sorrel gently on the top of its head.

The plump man stared at Lacy. "Had to foul Bothwell to put him down?"

"Pete!"

"You shut up, A-rab. I'm talkin' to this Lacy, here."

"Well I didn't *have* to, I guess," Lacy said. "But it sure helped."

Pierce threw back his head and laughed at that, and turned the sorrel and spurred it into a heavy canter. Angle Iron didn't seem too deep in fine cow-horses.

Behind them, Lacy heard the plump cowpoker, Pete, and the boy stirring up their mounts and following.

" 'It sure helped,' " Harry Pierce said, and laughed again. "The boys'll like that one." He glanced over his shoulder. "Don't mind old Pete, Lacy. Old Pete's just a natural son-of-a-bitch, is all."

Lacy's head was hurting again, and he had a belly ache to go with it. If Angle Iron didn't feed strangers coming in, and fine and pronto, he was likely to kill and cook him one fat son-of-a-bitch named Pete.


Pete was saved.

By a tin pie-plate full of red beans and onions, with chili peppers chopped up in it, and another pie-plate with hot corn bread and some strips of sow-belly on it.

A Mexican man with one eye did the cooking, in an open tin-roof walkway, with a sheet-iron griddle for the bread and pork meat, and a bean kettle on a rack over a brick-box fire.

A white woman served the food to Lacy. A big, bony woman, plain as a post, with sad brown eyes. She was wearing the biggest apron Lacy had ever seen. It had been sewn out of flour sacks, and read *Rally's Finest* across her front.

They'd come riding down on the ranch buildings in early afternoon, and Lacy'd seen the place was an old one—probably tried out up here well before the war. Burned out by the Comanches then, for sure, and rebuilt, maybe two or three times, as the Rangers and Comanches had fought the frontier back and forth.

There was an old pit-fort there, on a little rise. A mound of tamped earth, hard as rock after all these years, peeled cottonwood logs roofing the ditch, and gun slots just showing under the butts of the logs. There would have been another mound of packed earth over the cottonwood beams in the old days. A good fort for flat country. With the trouble these Angle Iron people seemed to be having, Lacy wondered why they didn't build that fort back up. Might come in handy did any riders come shooting into headquarters.

There was that old place, and three nice big stock corrals, a home house by the well—the house of nice finished lumber, too, that must have been freighted a fair 200 miles. A good barn, and a dog-leg stable, of rough lumber. In all, a first-class place, especially for north Texas. They seemed a little short in the men department, though. Nobody much around the place—the pokers'd be out on the range of course, working spring roundup from what Bud had said—but still, there was usually some pick-up help around headquarters on a busy ranch, wranglers, bronc-turners, and stablehands.

Not here.

Once Harry Pierce had let Lacy down from old Tiger, he and Pete—Peter Stern was his full name—and young Bud had gone to the south corral for remounts, and roped them out, with Bud getting third choice, a wall-eyed gray. Then they'd ridden out west, with Bud and the Australian looking back to give Lacy a wave where he was already sitting on the cook-shack bench, sniffing the smell of frying pork.

The bony woman hadn't seemed very surprised at their bringing him in. Must see considerable of saddletramps drifting through this country. She didn't seem very interested in Lacy's fight with Bothwell, either.

"More trouble," she'd said, and stalked off to get him his plate of beans. "Miss Louise," Harry Pierce had called her. Lacy'd seen a thousand women like her. On bust-out farms, in lumber camps, mining towns, cowtowns, on skinners' wagons, freighters' wagons, in laundry sheds and cookshacks. Worn-out women. Busted down by a dozen babies—and by beatings, too. But most of all, by trouble. By losing their husbands, and their children, and their homes, too, more often than not. To Indians, or saloon killings, sometimes. To weather or the eastern markets, mostly.

"Miss Louise" was another of them, with her sad eyes, and her bones, and her plain horse's face. Too plain even to make a cash-right whore, poor thing.

"You had enough to eat, Mister?" She was standing by the bench, waiting to put the tin plates into the wash bucket.

"Yes—and thank you kindly," Lacy said. "I was that hungry I could have chewed up a bear with his coat on."

That got a small smile out of her.

"If you're looking for work," she said, "there might be some." She took the plates away.

Lacy got up off the bench and walked after her. "I'm not much of a hand for cowpoking," he said.

She slid the plates into the wash bucket. "Too good for that, are you?" She didn't look up at him.

"No, I'm not," he said. "Just not much of a hand. I do pretty well with horses, though."

She straightened up and turned to face him, wiping her hands dry on the flour sack apron. "We will have a horse drive to do," she said, "but not yet."

Lacy saw she was younger than he'd thought. In her thirties somewhere, maybe. But she looked ten years older, and tired to death. "Well," he said, "I doubt I'll be staying around here, but otherwise I'd be glad enough to work that horse drive for you. What I would like, is to maybe buy a horse off of you people."

"Buy one?"

Lacy guessed he didn't look like much after a few weeks riding, and two days walking, and that dust-up with Bothwell. "Yes, ma'am, if you have one to sell."

The notion seemed to worry her, and she stood in the open walk-way shifting like a nervous horse, looking this way and that.

"Perhaps your husband could talk to me about it," Lacy said. "I can't afford a fine horse, but I guess I can pay a fair price for a decent animal."

She made a face. "We don't have a decent animal on the place." She looked straight at him. "Our horses, our *decent* horses were all stolen. The whole remuda. Stolen away five weeks ago, and two of our drovers killed."

"Sorry to hear that, ma'am." It explained why there was no bustle going on at the headquarters of Angle Iron. These

41

people were likely getting beat to death and stolen blind. Whatever the Central Cattle Company was, they seemed to have more pepper than these people—and for sure, more guns and money. Looked like his problem was going to be how to get into town, if these people couldn't let him have a horse.

"Is there a town near here, then, ma'am, where I might be able to buy a mount?"

"Bristolton." She wiped her hands on her apron again, and looked out over the ranch buildings. Then she looked at him. "Folks around here call it Pistoltown," she said.

"Oh, Lord, not another one of those," Lacy said, and this time roused a real smile out of her. Didn't help her looks much, though.

"Yes," she said. "It's a dangerous town." She was looking away, out to the range again, and at first, Lacy thought she might be waiting for someone, expecting some riders. Then he saw that it wasn't that. She was just shy, shy of strangers. Maybe worried what her husband would think of her standing talking to a drifter all day, if he should see her.

"Which way is that town, ma'am?" And you could bet a dollar to a doughnut, that the damn town was a good fifteen, twenty miles the other side of hell and gone.

"It's about eighteen miles south-east, Mister. . ."

There you are. "Lacy, ma'am."

"Mister Lacy." She started to put her hand out to shake, then thought better of that and put it down by her side.

She turned and started to walk away from him, going down the walkway toward the door to the house, but she stopped and called back, "Rudy will be going into town tomorrow. In the wagon, for wire and things. If you want to go, you can go with him." Then she turned and walked on to the door.

Once there, though, she stopped and looked back at him.

"If you want," she called, "you can stay in the bunk-house tonight." Then she went into the house and shut the door.

A nervous woman.

And she'd never told him her last name, either.

"What's her husband's name?" Lacy said to the Mexican cook. The one-eyed man didn't say anything, and Lacy started to ask him again in Spanish, but the man set the kettle back on its hook, and said, "She got no husband."

"Well, who owns the ranch?"

"The cook nodded to the door to the house. "She," he said.

"What's her name, then?"

"Bristol," the cook said.

"Oh, like the town. . ."

The cook nodded. "Her father make that town." He gave Lacy a narrow one-eyed look. Didn't like answering questions, it seemed.

"Well, you cook good beans," Lacy said.

"*Sí Señor*," said the cook, and commenced to stir them.

# CHAPTER FIVE

Most of the hands came riding in before dark. There weren't that many of them, maybe seven or eight. More than most ranches needed, but not many to work a spread the size of Angle Iron. And they weren't prime men. Or most of them weren't. The Australian, and maybe fat Pete Stern, were tough enough hands. And the foreman, Meager.

They'd come riding in with the sunset behind them, jogging along, going easy on tired horses. Lacy was sitting on the bunk-house steps, soaping his saddle and bridle leathers, and watched them ride in from the west. They didn't look like much of a bunch, even in the way they rode, except for the man in front. He looked like something considerable. Big. And he sat the saddle in an odd way.

When the horsemen were closer, Lacy saw that the lead rider *was* big. Damn near a giant, he looked like. And he rode with his upper body turned slightly. He was missing his left arm.

An old man in a rusty stovepipe hat. He wore a full beard that shone silver in the red sunset light. An *old* man, maybe seventy or more. He was dressed in a suit, too, the way some old-time cattlemen used to dress. A dusty, wrinkled, gray

44

suit, a dusty, wrinkled shirt that had been white once, and as he trotted into the corral yard and saw Lacy and pulled his tired roan over toward him, Lacy saw that he was wearing a Walker Colt's on his right hip. He was the only man Lacy had ever seen wearing one of those old cannons. A heavy-charge .44 that could down a grizzly, it was said.

The huge revolver looked small on this old man, though. Lacy figured him for one of the old Texas terrors—knew Sam Huston as a boy, rode with the first companies of Rangers, then (already an old man) rode with Hood in the war. He also figured him for the foreman, Mister Meager.

"My name's Meager," the old man said, looking down at Lacy as though he was a buffalo chip that rolled in on the wind. "Who in hell's blazes are you?"

Lacy stood up. "My name's Lacy, Mister Meager."

The old man rolled his eyes. They were wrinkled little eyes, black as an Indian's. "Oh, yes," he said. He had a clear high-pitched voice, like a younger man's. "The tramp who's supposed to have whipped Central's hard boy." He looked at Lacy as though he doubted it. "I suppose Miss Louise's already offered you a job here, and lodging?"

"Both," Lacy said.

"There'll be no job. I have no-accounts enough working on the place!" He turned his horse back toward the corrals, then called over his shoulder, "And if you expect to sit down to supper with Miss Louise looking like that, you have another think coming. You look like a damn farmer's pig! Get yourself washed and shaved—or don't come to the kitchen!" And he trotted off, sitting a little turned in the saddle, his white hair down to his shoulders. Even without the stovepipe hat, Lacy thought, the old man must stand well over six and a half feet. Maybe six-eight. His gnarled, spotted, work-broken hand had looked the size of a shovel on the reins.

An old Texas terror, no doubt.

And the kind of man to have his own spread, by now, and a rich one, at that—or be dead. And this one, this Mister Meager, wasn't dead by a long shot.

If a wash-up was the order of the day, Lacy thought he might as well get to it before the hands had finished unsaddling and currying and turning out their horses. The horses didn't look any better than the men, at least from the bunkhouse steps. Those rustlers—from the Cattle Company, no doubt—had choused Angle Iron out of every decent mount they had. What animals they'd gathered up in place looked pretty poor.

He walked into the bunkhouse, put the saddle and leathers down behind the small potbelly stove where he'd left his Sharps and bedroll, and dug in the bedroll for his other shirt, and a pair of under-drawers. If he was going fancy, he'd go fancy all the way.

He went out to the pump behind the bunkhouse, stripped down to his skin, and pumped a leaky bucket full of water for a soaking. He hadn't found any soap by the pump, so he used the saddle soap, and managed a fair lather with it, too. He soaped up his other dirty shirt and under-drawers while he was at it, and heard the first of the hands coming into the bunk-house behind him. He pumped his rinse water, then stepped nearer the back shelf, where he'd left the Bisley Colt, to do his rinsing.

It had been a long, long time since he'd felt comfortable standing stark naked without the Colt to hand. Not since he'd been fourteen years old, in fact.

None of the people came out to trouble him, though, and soon enough he'd dried himself with the old buckskin vest as well as he could, and dressed again, got his boots on, and buckled on the Colt. He reached down to slide the Arkansas toothpick out of his right boot, and saw that Bud Manugian was standing at the bunkhouse back door, watching him. The boy looked done in by a mighty hard day's work. Mister Meager doubtless didn't leave much slack when it came to cow-chores.

"Good evening, Lacy."

"Evening to you, Bud. Say, you have a piece of mirror I could borrow?"

"Sure do." And the boy ducked back into the bunkhouse and came out with a fairly big piece of glass, probably broken from some house mirror at one time. Lacy propped it up on a strip of lath on the bunkhouse wall, worked a little saddle soap into his still damp bristle of beard, and used the toothpick's slender double-edged blade to stroke the whiskers away.

"You always shave with that?"

Lacy lifted the long blade off his skin. "I do, when my razor hasn't been set and honed for a month or more. Less I feel I need a bleeding." He shaved carefully around the deep scar across his left cheek.

A face in a mirror. The most familiar thing there is. Familiar—and strange. Strange enough for most men—and women too—to talk to, if they were lonely enough. You'd talk to it, and damned if the reflection wouldn't answer you. Tell you what you wanted to hear, most times. Laugh along with you, too. Look at this, now. . .

Here's a man that's been around. . . that's seen the elephant. Not young, either; not with those weather-lines on his face, not with those touches of gray in his hair, not with a bullet-mark across his cheek like that. No, no young man looking in this mirror. Maybe a bad man, the mirror might think. But the glass wouldn't know how bad. Not unless it could see into a lot of other mirrors, from a lot of other years.

Mirrors that had had other men's faces in them. Women's faces, too. Forty dead men—or as near as made

47

no difference. And one dead woman.

One dead woman.

The face in the piece of mirror stared at him like a stranger.

I ought to have cut my fingers off, after I gunshot the first man, Lacy thought. Doing that would have been a smart thing to do.


Bud had introduced him around to the hands. A decent enough bunch of men, but hangdog, most of them. Damn few bright-and-comin'-at-you young cowpokers among them. Most had something wrong with them: a man named Clark had a wry neck; a boy named Norwood seemed near half-witted; a fellow named Rudy Snell looked sixty if he was a day—and still trying to do a drover's full day's work. There was something wrong with almost every one of them.

Pete Stern didn't have much to say. Nothing to say to Lacy. Stern looked fit enough for the work, even though he was fat. And the Australian, Pierce, would have made a good hand on any lash-up.

Lacy didn't have to ask where the class hands were. The answer would be: run off, or bought off, by the Central Cattle Company. Chased out, or hired on at foreman's wages to work the Company's other spreads. The Australian hadn't chased, though, and fat Pete Stern hadn't run, either, not yet. Lacy doubted that any of the Company's people had been foolish enough to even approach old man Meager. He looked the sort to take that Walker .44 to any man who looked sideways at him. Must have been a rare thunderstorm of a man when he was young.

"Say," Lacy said to Harry Pierce while all of them were drifting over the corral yard toward the kitchen walk. "Mister Meager strikes me as more of an owner, than a foreman."

The Australian laughed. "Don't he though," he said. "I'd take him for a rare old range king, myself."

"Always been foreman, though?"

"Oh, no. He did have a place, I hear, long time back. Down at Lockhart. Say his wife and boys were killed on the place, and that was the end of it for him. Poor old sod."

"Indians."

"Oh, no. American troops. Yankee troops, during your war."

They walked along for a minute, not saying anything. The sun was down now; only faint streaks of dull red still lay along the western horizon. Everything around the men, the men themselves, had the dim silvery look of last daylight, coming dark. Their shirts, their bandannas, their faces, all looked dust gray.


The cook had set up a long plank table with benches beside the kitchen walk, and when the hands gathered round, the Mexican brought a kettle of beans to the table, and then a stack of hot loaves of bread. It smelled damn good. Then he brought two kerosene lanterns and set them out. The hands didn't sit down though, they just stood around the table sniffing at the smoke from the bean-pot. Waiting for old Meager, Lacy thought.

Just so.

The house door opened, and the old man came stomping down the walk with Miss Louise right behind him. Meager pulled out a crack-back kitchen chair at the head of the table, seated her, and stomped to the far end and sat down. Then the hands took to the benches; Lacy elbowed himself a place between Bud and a cowboy named Parsons, and saw that nobody was reaching. Waiting for a blessing.

Meager gave it, called it out loud in his young man's voice.

"Oh, loving Lord, we beg thee to bless this good food here—that these dull and lazy hands are goin' to gobble and get pig fat on! And we thank you for that blessing, Lord—and goodbye!"

The Mexican piled a stack of tin plates on the table—had held off before this waiting on the blessing, Lacy thought—and the men passed them around. Then Miss Louise took a piece from a loaf of bread, and served herself a spoonful of beans. Then the men went for it.

The men ate hard, and Lacy kept well up with them. There wasn't much in the way of conversation. When the last of the beans were gone, the Mexican brought on a plate of fried steaks to follow up. It was good eats, right along. Whatever troubles Angle Iron was having with its fences, horses, and punchers, the ranch still set a solid table.

There was some talk while the steaks were going down, generally talk of ranch work—shop, they called it—concerning steers, calves, cow ponies, hard rides and hard falls. They'd lost a man last week with a broken leg in a *barranca* on the north range. ("Damn fool, and no loss," old Meager said.) And the paint mare called Topsy had dropped a fine-legged foal. ("Good mare," Bud Manugian told Lacy. "Best horse on the place, now.")

"Lost any cattle?"

"Hell no!" Meager broke in. The old man had sharp ears. "Those God-damned sons-of-bitches—your pardon, Miss Louisa—those God-damned sons-of-bitches see no need to steal now what they'll get anyway when they steal the whole damned ranch!"

"They took your horses, though."

"To cripple us," Meager said, and the old man waggled the empty-sleeved stump of his left arm at Lacy, "that's why they stole the horses, not for the value of the beasts." He had his fried steak clutched in the fingers of his one hand, and he tore another chunk out of it with teeth the size and color of a horse's.

"Miss Louise mentioned you people were driving some replacement horses up. . ."

"Miss Louise," Meager said, raising his voice, "shouldn't be blabbin' ranch business to every saddle-tramp that comes in for free eats!"

At the far end of the table, the woman looked up at that and Lacy saw her face redden in the lamplight.

"You hear me, Miss Bristol?" the old man called down the table.

"I suppose the night herders could hear you, Mister Meager," she said, and went back to her eating.

The old man let that rest, and gave Lacy a sharp look. "You wouldn't be a Company man yourself, now, would you, Lacy? Come walkin' out here to give us some trouble of one kind or another?"

"No," Lacy said, "I'm not."

"And might a man have your word of honor for that?"

"Yes," Lacy said. "You have my word of honor." He felt sorry for the old man. To have lived so past his time—past the time when "word of honor" meant what it said.

"Very well." Meager said, "And I suppose you want a job?"

"No, thank you, Mister Meager. I'll be going into town in the morning. Not that I don't appreciate the offer, but—"

"I don't need to know your reasons, sir! Or your business! Certainly you're free to go when and where you wish!" The old man tore out another chunk of steak, and chewed it with considerable satisfaction, his mouth open, teeth shining in the lamplight, silver beard wagging.

"You should have let the drifter walk, A-rab!" Pete

Stern said from down the other side of the table. " 'Stead of us be bringin' him in for a free feed."

"Scared he'll take something out of your mouth, Pete?" Harry Pierce said. Some other men laughed. Lacy was surprised when Stern laughed, too. "Like to see him try," the fat man said. "I'd—"

"That's enough rough talk," old Meager said, and the men were quiet. "We have a lady at table."

Harry Pierce chewed and swallowed a last bite of steak, and stood up. "Sorry ma'am," he said to Louise Bristol, "You excuse me, I'll be taking grub out to the night herd."

"Of course, Harry," the woman said, "You go on."

"And mind how you go, Pierce," old Meager said. He glanced at Lacy. "Seems Bothwell was whipped in earnest." He leaned over to Lacy. "We thought that fight a possible ruse, young man. So mind how you go. Bothwell will be wanting his own back!"

"Sir." The Australian walked off toward the corrals, and some of the other men got up to go as well.

"Are you waiting for a sweet, sir?" Meager said to Lacy. "Dessert?"

"I guess not," Lacy said, and started to get up from the table.

"Sweets are bad for the belly, sir! A knife in your gut—that's your sweet dessert, sir!" He stood up, tall as a tower in the lamplight, and bowed down to the table to Louise Bristol. "Pardon me, ma'am, for saying *belly* in your presence."

# CHAPTER SIX

Lacy woke just before dawn.

He'd bunked down in the last cot against the far wall, and when he woke, he could barely make out the row of cots along each wall, the figures of the cowpokers snoring out the last of their sleep. The cook would be ringing the triangle soon, getting them up and out.

He snaked his hand under the pillow, checking on the Colt. Its deep-curved Bisley grip was warm from his sleeping on it. He threw back the sweat smelling blanket, swung his feet to the floor, and stood up, stretching hard in the darkness, feeling the muscles in his back tighten, then give with the strain. His joints cracked a little as he stretched, reaching for low plank ceiling. He stood on his toes, and his fingertips touched it. One of the cow-hands snorted in his sleep, and turned over with a sigh.

Lacy pulled his folded trousers out from under the thin horsehair mattress and stepped into them. He left his boots off; too noisy to stomp around in them this early. He padded down the bunkhouse between the rows of cots, opened the back door—the rusted hinges sqwawked like hens—and stepped down into the yard.

Dark and cool, with the coolness that in Texas passes like a breath before the heat of the day. The darkness was just graying to light. He picked a big chipped basin off the bench along the bunkhouse wall, walked to the pump, and looked for the priming bucket. It was empty. To save himself the walk around to one of the watering troughs, he tried the pump handle. It rattled and squeaked empty the first two strokes, then spat out a short jet of water. After that, it pumped out gushing. He filled the basin, set it on the rickety split-leg stand, and commenced washing his face, sluicing the cold water down his chest and armpits. He buried his face in the basin, opening his eyes into the dull dawn light under the water. Then he straightened up snorting, spitting out a mouthful of water, blinking it out of his eyes.

Something hit him very hard in the side. Hard enough to knock him against the basin-stand and push it over.

"How about some room there, Dad?"

Pete Stern.

Lacy turned, and stepped away from the fallen stand. Stern must have elbowed him hard; his side hurt like hell. Must have damn near cracked a rib.

Another man, then, might have turned and gone for Stern blind, in a rage at being sneak hurt that way, and might have tangle-footed in the basin-stand doing it, too. And Stern was looking for that, for a surprised man to jump right back at him without thinking about it. The fat man was braced for it, set, his thick arms up, a big right fist cocked.

Lacy stepped another step back, catching his breath where his ribs pained him.

Stern thought he was backing off.

"That how you whipped that back-shooter, Bothwell?"

54

he said. "Backin' him to death?" He laughed. "No hard feelin's, Dad. Just you pick up that basin and pump me some water, we'll call it even-steven." He was smiling, still standing braced for trouble, but with his hands at his sides. He looked to be built like a boar hog, squat and thick with lard in the dirty red long-johns he was wearing. Lacy saw he was barefoot, too. Likely had seen Lacy go out, and decided to follow him and pick his fight.

Lacy moved to the side, starting to circle. "Uh-oh—old Dad's goin' to fight." Stern smiled. He looked like a Dutchman with his pale skin and bulging blue eyes. Past his shoulder, Lacy saw men standing in the bunkhouse door. The commotion had gotten them up.

It seemed to Lacy that Stern was one of those men who loved a fist-fight. It was not so common as people thought. Lacy'd known men who'd rather gun fight than fist-fight any day. Something awful personal about hitting a man in the face. . .

"You circle Bothwell to death? That what you did?" Stern saw the other men at the bunkhouse door. "Guess this drifter just backed and circled old Bothwell plumb to sleep!" He laughed at his own joke—and came at Lacy with a jump.

By then, Lacy was breathing easier, taking deep breaths without the ribs hurting him so much. He wasn't surprised when the cowboy came at him. He was surprised the fat man was that fast.

Stern got to him, and hit him a hard punch in the belly before Lacy danced back out of the rush.

"Come on!" Stern said with a grunt—and came at him again.

Lacy went to meet him.

There was a difference between them then, that only the Australian, Pierce, saw and understood.

Stern was fighting, punching, to hurt—to knock Lacy down.

Lacy was hitting hard enough to kill.

Pierce had seen that kind of hitting before.

Stern was a tough man. Lacy had hit him very hard, had broken his nose and knocked two of his teeth out but the cowboy was still on his feet, still coming on. Stern wasn't the boxer that Bothwell had been, but he was strong as a horse.

Lacy stepped in as Stern came at him again, then jumped to the side, swung, and caught the cowboy under the ear. Stern staggered, turned, and came on again. Blood was pouring down out of his nose.

If Lacy'd had his boots on, he could have kicked the man down. No boots.

Lacy put his head down and drove into Stern's belly to butt him down. Stern staggered back, and Lacy hit him in the belly, left and right, as hard as he could. Hit him as if he could tear through that fat and muscle with his fists, and kill the man. It was like punching into india rubber. The cowboy grunted as the punches hit him.

But he didn't go down.

The other cow-pokers were yelling and cheering them on, starting to hustle into a rough circle to ring the fight. Lacy was starting to run out of wind. His head was hurting again where Bothwell had hit him the day before. If it hadn't hurt so much, it would have been funny. He shook his head to clear it, and moved back to get a good breath of air. He saw Pete Stern, his red longjohns spattered with redder blood, pawing the air with his big fists, lumbering after him. Behind the cowboy, Lacy saw the other men, their mouths open, yelling, howling for blood. He couldn't tell, from the noise, whose they were yelling for.

It should have been funny. God knows the Earps would

have loved to see it. Doc, too. It would have made their day to see Dodge City's Dashing Dan, the whores' delight, Mister Silk Shirt, himself—an old man with gray in his hair, scarred like a falling-down rummy—waltzing around a ranch yard in a fist-fight with a fat cowboy in red underwear.

It should have been funny.

Stern, squealing like a wounded boar, rushed him again, swung and missed, swung again as Lacy ducked away, and hit him in the jaw. Lacy stumbled and almost fell. He heard Bud Manugian yelling to him, and he kept his feet and kept moving. He saw the wooden basin-stand—no use to him. He saw the big basin in the dirt, bent, and picked it up as he moved.

He turned as Stern came at him again, and swung the basin sideways into the fat man's head.

It rang.

Stern stopped moving, and put his hands up to cover his head. The blue eyes seemed to bulge more than ever.

Lacy stepped in again, swinging the heavy basin in both hands. It landed on Stern's head, on his fingers, with a clang.

Stern yowled with pain, stumbling back, shaking his mashed fingers, and Lacy went after him, spinning in a half circle and swinging the basin down onto the cowboy's head with all his strength. The basin rang out like a church-bell as it struck—and Pete Stern's eyes rolled back into his head, and he dropped like a dead man into the dirt.


Lacy was afraid that the old man might die.

Meager stood propped up against the bunkhouse wall, his face tomato red, wheezing and gurgling with laughter. He'd begun by roaring, and was now reduced to the wheezes. It didn't look healthy for the old man to be so red in the face. Lacy thought he might have an apoplexy or something like that.

"You—you—" The old man started wheezing again. "You sure have a . . . a style . . . of fightin'! Hit a man with a. . .a bowl!" He straightened up, leaning against the bunkhouse wall. "Damn. . . damn if it didn't sound like the bell in the Methodist chapel in Galveston!" He wheezed. "I thought it was time to go to church!"

No hard feelings among the Angle Iron hands, or their foreman, about Pete Stern getting clubbed cold with a wash basin. They all seemed to take it as a better than fair joke on old Pete. The men had lugged Stern back into the bunkhouse. "Put him back to bed, boys," Meager had called, "ole Pete's plumb wore out puttin' dents in that there wash pan!"

Meager had come steaming around the back of the bunkhouse to kick out the hands for not jumping to the cook's triangle, had heard the yelling, and had the good fortune to see the last of the fight. It had made the old man's day, no doubt about it.

"What the tarnation did you hit poor Bothwell with, boy? A washboard?" He'd hauled himself up on his big roan one-handed, reached down to settle the Walker Colt on his hip, then leaned from the saddle to shake hands with Lacy. "Take a brave man to fight you in a kitchen, boy," he'd said, his huge, gnarled hand gripping Lacy's like a steam press. *"Vaya con Dios."* Then he'd turned his horse to ride with the others.

Lacy stood by the corral watching them ride out. Bud turned in his saddle to wave goodbye. They'd be late getting out to the herd this morning, thanks to a damnfool fat cowboy and a scarface drifter. One long fight and one short breakfast—and on their way.

On their way to nowhere. The Central Cattle Company would see to that.

There had been a day—a considerable time ago—when a set-up like this would have looked real ripe. Ripe as a damson plum. The Bothwells were likely good enough, but not as good as a young gunman in a buckskin vest had been. Not as ready to step in and get it over, maybe. Not as ready to see that Meager, the old man, was all that was holding this lash-up together. Not as quick to call that old man out, and it wouldn't take much calling with an old he-alligator like Meager. Call him out, and kill him. The young man in his fine bleached-white buckskin vest would have gotten it done in jig-time.

Jig-time.

And could do it still. Could get a piece of the action from Central—and show the gate to the Bothwells. No wallowing around in the dirt with a fat cowboy with a bloody nose. None of that. And he'd see the look on all their faces. That look. . .

That look that said, *Be careful of this man. He holds the life of any man he faces in his hand.*

A respectful look. It would only cost one huge old man, lying on his face in the street in Pistoltown. And there had been a time he'd have done it.

Worse times, even, than these.

He walked back to the bunkhouse to see if Pete Stern was waking up yet. It made a funny sound, to knock a man down with a wash pan. But the man was down and out, just the same. Could up and die from it, just the same.

Stern was awake, stretched out on his cot with old Rudy Snell moping at his face with a wet rag. Louise Bristol was sitting on the next cot beside that, holding Pete's hand. She looked up at Lacy when he came in to the bunkhouse, and it was a cold look.

Lacy walked over to the cot. Stern rolled his eyes at him, but didn't say anything. Snell had got all the blood off Stern's face, but his red long-johns were stiff with it, all down the front. His nose was badly swollen, and bruised black across the bridge where Lacy had broken it, and his lower lip had been cut where he'd lost the teeth.

He looked even worse that Lacy felt. Lacy's head was beating like an Indian drum.

"That was a good fight," Lacy said to him. "Sorry I had to hit you with that basin, but it was the only way I could knock you down."

Stern glared up at him, opened his mouth, and winced at the pain of the split lip. "Without you hit me with that thing, I'd have whipped you good!" he said. "May do it yet." He sounded like a man with a bad cold.

"Well," Lacy said. "You'd have sure wore me to a frazzle." He sat down beside Louise Bristol on the next cot. "You were a sight harder to handle than Abe Bothwell, I'll tell you that." And it happened that he had been, too.

That appeared to make Pete Stern feel somewhat better about things.

"Huh?" he said.

"Hold on a minute, now," Lacy said. "Let me take a look at your eyes." He got up and bent over Stern.

"What in hell for?"

"See if your center pupils—the little round black parts—are both the same size. If they are, it means your brains aren't scrambled on you."

"Huh?" But he goggled up at Lacy in some apprehension.

Lacy looked carefully, and took off his hat to shade Stern's face from the morning sunlight glowing through the bunkhouse windows. Then he took the hat away, and watched Stern's pupils slowly expand again. Both the same size.

"Looks good," he said.

"What do you know? You ain't no doctor." But Stern looked pleased, none the less.

"A doctor told me about that."

"Huh?"

Louise Bristol gave Lacy a friendlier look. She patted Stern's hand, and stood up. "I've got to be gettin' over to the kitchen now, Pete, if me and Manuel are goin' to be bakin' you that peach pie."

Stern pouted like a baby. He still held onto her hand.

"You do want that pie, don't you? Before Mister Meager and the boys ride in? You know how Mister Meager holds against sweets."

"Now, Pete," Snell said, "I'll stick here with you; we ain't goin' to leave you alone, boy."

"Huh?"

"Mister Lacy," Louise Bristol said, "I'd appreciate a word with you." She patted Stern's hand again and he let go. "And this pie's goin' to be just for you, Pete. Nobody else is goin' to get a bite unless you say so."

Lacy walked beside her out across the yard. The hard, bright morning light didn't favor her. It showed her plainness cruelly. She was a big woman, only a few inches shorter than Lacy.

"Did you mean what you said about the pupils of his eyes?"

"A doctor told me that, yes."

"Well, thank the Lord for that." She shook her head. "They're all like rough children, these drovers. Like little boys. Helpless as children, too, sometimes." She glanced up at him and smiled. "I guess," she said, "I baby them because I don't have children of my own to raise."

Then Lacy saw why the Bothwells hadn't yet killed old

man Meager. It was because that wouldn't be enough to break Angle Iron after all.

They'd have to kill the woman, too.

# CHAPTER SEVEN

Lacy sat at the long kitchen table, watching while Louise Bristol and Manuel made up the pie dough and rolled it out. The cook opened a can of peaches for the filling, and they made the pie and slid it into the brick oven standing beside the big iron range. It was hot beside the oven, even this early in the day, even out in the open kitchen walkway. The walkway was roofed over with trash wood and split planks, just something to keep the sun off, but bright spots and streaks of sunlight came through the rough planking anyway, to speckle in bright yellow the packed dirt and long table, the sagging wood cabinets of plates and pots and pans, butcher knives, serving spoons, and chipped enamel cups. The squat brick oven, the wide black range, were spotted like a Mexican tiger.

"Would you like to come into the house, Mister Lacy?"

She was looking down at him, dusting her hands on her apron.

Lacy got up and followed her down the walk. He didn't want to take much time talking with her. It was late morning already, and a lot of miles to go to get to town.

Town, a decent horse, a cool beer. . . Then he'd ride out.

South, into old Mexico.

The main house looked as nice on the inside as on the out. Done up in real style, especially for a north Texas ranchhouse. The big room had a carpet on the floor, red, with blue flowers, and there was a fine deep-bottom arm chair, and side tables, and tall standing oil lamps wherever someone might sit down and do close work, or read. There was a big, blue-stone hearth at the other end of the room, with cooking irons swung into the fireplace. Probably used it for winter cooking in the old days. Now they must tack up boards to close in the walkway.

A very handsome house. Glass panes in the windows, too, Lacy noticed. Time must have been when Angle Iron was important in this Panhandle country. When the Bristols were important.

"Do sit down, Mister Lacy."

Lacy sat down in a straight-back chair beside a small table with a stereoscope on it.

"I believe," Louise Bristol said, sitting opposite him in the armchair, "you told me you'd worked with horses, Mister Lacy." She looked something like a horse herself, with her sad brown eyes and long nosed, long jawed face.

"Yes, ma'am, I have worked with horses."

"Well," she said, her fingers nervously pleating a fold in her apron, "I believe that Mister Meager has allowed that we're going to be driving a replacement herd up from Lockhart. Replacement for the animals that were stolen from us."

"Yes, ma'am."

She raised her eyes and looked at him directly, then, and Lacy saw how angry she was, under the shyness.

"The animals that were stolen. . . and those two boys

shot dead." She stopped talking for a moment, and went back to pleating her apron.

"Would you care for work on that drive, Mister Lacy?" she asked, looking down at her apron. "We would pay, I believe, a better than fair wage for the work."

"I appreciate the offer, ma'am, but I'll have to be moving on, so I must refuse it." Not picking up Angle Iron's hot potato. That's flat.

She smoothed her apron down, and looked up. "Well, now, perhaps you might reconsider, Mister Lacy. We've managed the spring round up already, and we won't be going for the horses till next month. I think—"

Lacy shook his head." I regret, ma'am, I just won't be able to do it." The Company must be squeezing hard for her to have to almost beg him this way. And not just for a wrangler's job, either. The two fist-fights—and likely old Meager's sharp eye—had branded him a fighting man, or at least some sort of hard case. Louise Bristol was looking for more help than a yippee and a dally-loop on that drive. And she was right to look, too. No way would the Central Cattle Company let that fresh horse herd through from Lockhart. Not without shooting.

Angle Iron had managed its spring round up, and it had broken their bottom-of-the-barrel nags right down. Bud's pony, Blacky, had been about average, after all.

Oh, they'd need guns on that drive, no doubt. More guns than they'd ever get. And this sad plain lady was still looking at him.

"Miss Bristol. . . pardon me for asking. . . but don't you have some family? Some men who could come and side you in this business?"

She didn't say anything for a moment, and Lacy thought she might not have cared for his question. Then she said,

"I. . . I have no family now. . . except for Mister Meager. He was my grandfather's friend, you see. He married my grandfather's sister."

"No younger men?" Lacy said, as if any of this was his business.

"I had a nephew," she said, "Martin Bristol." There were tears in her eyes, now. "He was one of the two that was killed when they stole our horses." She wiped her eyes with the hem of her apron. "A boy seventeen years old. . . they. . . they shot him. . .and while he was lyin' hurt on the ground, they put a rope onto him. . .and dragged him to death." She held up her head and blinked away the tears. "Mister Meager read the signs."

"I see," Lacy said. And indeed he did.

"Mister Meager intended then to go riding straight down to San Antonio, and go into the offices of the Company there, and kill those men in their office, that had caused this to happen." She stared at Lacy as though she was asking him for something she had to have. "But I couldn't let that old man do that, could I? *Could I?* They would have had the police kill him in that city, a poor wild one-armed old man like that." She looked down and began fiddling with her apron again. "I got down on my knees to Mister Meager. I begged him on my knees not to go, not to leave us alone. I begged him on my knees, and he finally said he wouldn't."

Then she sat quiet; she had no more to say.

*Not to leave us. . .us.* Then Lacy realized what she meant. She and the hands, those busted-down and busted-out cowpokers of hers.

"I wish I could help you, ma'am." Just don't, for the love of God, get down on your knees to me.

But the crying—and the begging—were over with. Louise Bristol sniffed a couple of times, smoothed her apron, and stood up. "Well," she said, "if you can't, you can't; and that's that. I expect we'll manage."

Lacy stood up, and she led the way to the door. "Are you sure you wish to leave before the pie is done?" she said. "Won't be much longer, and I doubt that Peter will be up to eatin' the whole thing." Lacy opened the door for her and followed her out.

She turned to him and smiled, homely as a hedge fence. "Manuel makes a fine peach pie when Mister Meager is safely off the place!"

Lacy laughed, and bowed to her like a gentleman. "It will be my loss, ma'am, I'm sure, but the sooner I'm in town, the better."

"Very well," she said. "If you'll go and fetch Rudy Snell, I'll give him the list, and he can hitch the wagon and be on his way." She held out her hand to shake.

She had a strong grip.

"Good luck, ma'am," Lacy said.

"My father, Emmet Charles Bristol, used to say: Bristols need no luck. They make their own."


Snell was a slow driver.

But since the team looked to be slow goers, anyway, it likely didn't make any difference. The day had turned into a Texas spring scorcher, after all. Lacy'd been north so long, he'd forgotten how personal the Texas sun felt, when it beat down on you.

The buffalo grass stretched out on either side of the wagon ruts that served this country for a trail, tall as Indiana bluestem and burning gold in the sunshine. No saying this wasn't prime cattle country. It was. Just as it had been buffalo country twenty years before. Comanche country.

"No Indian trouble in this country?"

"Aw, naw," Snell said. "Not since the Army busted them 'em up in the seventies." He hawked up a goober, and spit just off-side the wheel-horse's ear. "They're around. Lot of 'um on the reservation now. Wild ones stay way out, mostly, 'cept when they come through huntin'."

"Been hunting now around here, Bud Manugian said."

"That's so. They comb out the game pretty brisk, but you still don't see 'em." He clucked at the team, and they stepped out from a slow walk to a faster slow walk. "Wouldn't care to meet any of the young bucks out in the lonesome, myself. Comanche are sudden Indians. . ."

Sudden Indians. Lacy'd known a sudden old Indian. An old Shoshone with a Parker shotgun. Sudden for sure, and a good friend as well.

Not always such good memories of Indians. Lacy'd fought them once, Cheyennes, in the Dakotas. It had been a bad time, nothing like what he'd heard men talk about as Indian fighting. The men he'd been with had been territorial militia. Good men, most of them, and led by an ex-Union officer named Perkins. He was a good man, as well. Knew his business, and hadn't made a fuss about it.

And in weeks of riding the country, they had not once met the Cheyennes in battle. Had only seen Cheyennes twice in the daylight, in fact.

Of the twenty-three men riding in their troop, nine were killed during the campaign. None of them in what you'd call fighting.

They were just shot.

Several killed in the daytime. Just riding along down in some rain-soaked gully with slickers keeping them as sweat-wet as the rain might have. Then a shot—a rifle shot from a considerable distance—and Billy Chetwin rolled out of his saddle with his jaw shot away. Gobbling. . . tongue flapping out. . .drowning in his own blood.

Some killed at night, too. Might have been a time when Indians didn't fight at night. Those Cheyennes didn't seem to mind it, though.

Lacy had killed two Indians in that campaign. One, he crept up on at a campfire, and knifed the man to death. Sometimes he thought that Indian may have been sick, and left behind alone because of that. He'd been sitting wrapped in a blanket by a small fire. Lacy'd come down on him and cut his throat like a calf's.

The other man he'd shot with a rifle, and that just by luck. He'd fired at a file of Indians riding through some willow trees by a creek; a shot from a distance of several hundred yards. He and the men with him had yelled with surprise when one of the Indians had fallen off his horse.

They'd charged on the Indians at a gallop, and driven them off before they could pick up their wounded. Lacy and the miltiamen with him hadn't fired another shot, and the Cheyennes hadn't fired either. They'd just ridden off.

The man Lacy shot was still alive when they rode up. He was a short, tired-looking Indian with bow legs. Lacy had shot him in the hip, and a piece of white bone was poking out there in the blood. The man was lying on his side, resting his head on his bent arm. He watched Lacy and the others get off their horses and walk over to him. He didn't seem to think very much of them.

Now that the militia had him, they weren't sure what to do with him. Lacy wished that Captain Perkins was there to decide it. One of the men who'd been talking some about scalping, didn't want to do it now that the Indian was lying there looking at him.

They decided to kill him instead of taking him prisoner, partly because he was hurt so bad. Captain Perkins had wanted a prisoner, but this man had a piece of broken bone sticking out of him. The idea of getting him on a horse seemed mighty unpleasant.

They decided to shoot him.

Lacy did it.

It was one of the first payments he ever had to make for his reputation as a pistol fighter.

Lacy had shot Indians after that, in other years, in other parts of the country. But these had been personal fights, not part of a damn campaign, a damn war. From what he saw in that little war in the Dakotas, Lacy decided that the Civil War must have been just the same—just longer, bigger, and noisier. It explained to him why veterans of the war were sometimes half crazy.

Four years campaigning in the Dakotas would have damn well made him mad as a hatter.

"There's a rider comin' on." Old Snell sounded worried.

Lacy saw a man riding a gray horse, way down the track. It was too far to make the man out, but he had no rifle in his hands.

"Do you know him?"

"Too damn far to tell," Snell said. "I don't know that horse."

Lacy stretched back into the wagon-bed to reach the Sharps out of its scabbard. He held the big rifle across his lap. Then he reached down and eased the rawhide keeper-loop off the hammer of his holstered Colt.

"You tell me if you recognize him as he comes up."

"I will," Snell said. His voice had a tremor in it. He was too old and tired a man for trouble. Odd about age, Lacy thought. Old man Meager'd be breathing fire and yearning for a fight if he was driving the wagon.

The man on the gray was riding straight up the track toward them. Still no rifle in his hands. And Lacy began to relax as he saw that the man wasn't sitting tight on his horse, being careful to keep him collected for trouble. The man was riding loose as a goose.

"Shit," Snell said, "that's the lawyer! But I sure never saw that horse before."

"What lawyer?"

"Name's Talbot. A stuck-up dude is all he is."

Lacy'd known lawyers who were handy with a gun. "Not a bad man, is he?"

"Shit, no," Snell said. "That dude couldn't hit a bull in the ass with a bass fiddle. Never pushed nobody that I ever heard off."

Lacy hefted the Sharps and stretched back to slide it into its scabbard. When he straightened up, he saw that the rider was waving to them, riding on in.

Then Lacy looked at the horse.

# CHAPTER EIGHT

It was a slate-gray gelding, and looked about as big as a house. Looked young. Thoroughbred for sure, with some Morgan, probably. Long-legged as an English hunter, but with more chest, heavier quarters.

A beautiful horse.

The rider was a big, broad-shouldered, red-faced man. A drinker, Lacy thought, and probably some younger than he looked. Wearing a dude's brown plaid suit, and black city Stetson.

"Howdy," the lawyer said, and he reined the big gray in beside the wagon. "You boys wll be Iron hands, I suppose."

"That's right," Snell said, "we are."

"Miss Bristol is at the ranch, then?"

"That's her business, Mister."

"She's out there," Lacy said.

The lawyer tipped his hat to him. "Thank you, sir. Pleasure to meet a gentleman here, out on the wide plains of Texas."

Lacy saw that the man was drunk. Holding it well

enough, when he kept his mouth shut. It occurred to him that Talbot might have more to say, if asked.

"Legal business sending you out this way, Mister Talbot?" He gave the man a friendly smile. "I understand you're an attorney."

Snell snorted, but Talbot ignored him.

"I do have the privilege, sir, of being an officer of the court. The infrequent circuit court, in this case, of the benighted township of Bristolton."

"Named so, I understand, for Miss Bristol's father," Lacy said.

"Or her grandfather, sir. Yes, that's correct. The family's gone downhill since those days, however."

"Talbot," old Snell said, brave enough now, "you watch out how you talk about Miss Louise."

"Oh, no offense. No offense," the lawyer said. "Miss Louise is a lady." He tipped his hat in a general way, as if she were present. "A very lucky lady, if I may say so."

"How is that, counsellor?" Lacy said. Snell hawked and spat.

"Why, I'm the bearer of a striking offer to her for the sale of her property," Talbot said. He stopped talking then, and sat his horse staring at Lacy. His face got redder. "It will very soon be common knowledge, of course. Nothing confidential about it." He straightened up in his saddle.

"Well, we surely won't talk about it," Lacy said. "None of our business. Would be nice, though, if something good came to Miss Louise. I suppose the Central people would be bound to do right by her. . ."

"Yes. Yes." Talbot reined his horse clear of the wagon. "Well, I have to be getting on. The lady's at the ranch, you say?"

"Yes."

"Well, I have to be getting on." He gave them a little

wave with his right hand, and trotted off up the track, heading out for Angle Iron.

"Drunk as a skunk," Snell said, and clucked to the team to get them moving.

"Rouse those horses up a little," Lacy said. "I want to get to town before the damn moon comes up." He was still turned, watching the lawyer ride off, watching the paces of the gray. It had been a long time since he had wanted a particular horse that bad. It was strange; it was almost like needing a particular woman. He had the feeling it wouldn't have bothered him much to kill the lawyer for that horse.

Now a fist-fighter, coming up on being a horsethief. He was training himself up into something prime, no doubt about it. . .

They got to Bristolton by moonrise.

Snell pulled the team up at the crest of a low, brushy ridge. The track, wider, more heavily rutted now, curved away down into the town, turned onto Main Street.

Bristolton was bigger than Lacy had thought. He'd figured a mighty small cow-town: a saloon or two, a general store, a livery and freight outfit. Three or four little family houses north of the line.

No such thing. Bristolton was a cowtown, all right, but it wasn't all that small. The false-front buildings ran a good stretch down the main drag, with kerosene lamps strung along the high boardwalks on either side. The moonlight showed the rest of the town up well enough. There were two other dirt streets running north and south of Main, with houses and shops and corrals lined up and down them. The south side, as usual, looked to be the most lively. More lanterns on that street, more people in the street, too. Lacy could hear music.

"It looks like a railroad town."

Snell was pleased at the compliment. "Don't it? It does for sure look like it's got the railroad, but it don't. The railroad's still stuck way outside Amarillo. Nope, that down there is pure old-timey beef-town, Mister Lacy! All the herds for a hundred miles come in here to drive north. And that's a lot of cows!"

"I thought the railroads had cut the long drives right out from down here."

"Hell, they could, I suppose," Snell said, and clucked his team on down the ridge. "If they wasn't so busy cuttin' each other's throats."

They rode on down the ridge, once the bank of an old river that had dried up and blown away long ago. Snell reined the team around a parked freight-wagon, forcing two horsemen coming toward them to ride wide. For so late, there were a fair number of people up and doing.

"Hey, Snell!" a man called from the opposite board-walk. Snell raised his whip and waggled it. "That's Pillsbury," he said to Lacy. "Worse drunk in town. And that's sayin' something, I can tell you!" He pulled up the team. "Well, now, this here's the livery us Iron people use. I'll be bunkin' up in the loft; loadin' and movin' out in the mornin'. I don't suppose Nathan Brittles'd mind your bunkin' in here too. Specially, when he hears you whipped Abe Bothwell."

"I guess not," Lacy said. "I think I'll try for a bed down the south side." He swung down from the wagon seat, and grunted at the ache and stiffness in his butt and back from the long day's wagoneering. He reached in over the plank side for his saddle and bedroll and rifle. "Much obliged for the lift, though," he said. "And say, Snell, what's the nicest whorehouse in town?"

"Damn," said Snell, up on the wagon seat, grinning and

shaking his head. "You young bulls don't never quit thinkin' about it, do you?"

"Not so young anymore, Rudy, but I try to keep it in mind, just the same."

"Well, I'll tell you, I can't do a damn thing anymore, but if I could, well I'd go to Miss Susan Maynard's. If I had the money. Miss Susan is a real nice lady, and from what I hear, her girls are as good as ever."

"Thanks, Rudy, I'll give it a try." Lacy hoisted the saddle on one shoulder, the bedroll on the other. He held the rifle case in his right hand.

Snell turned the team into the big, open double doors of the livery. The entrance was dark. A single safety-lantern burned dimly deep in the back of the building.

First the team, then Snell, then the wagon passed inside, into the dark.

"Goin' to cost you, though!" Snell's voice from the darkness.


South Street was narrower than Main, the same rutted dirt, and crowded in on both sides by lamplit cribs, and sheds and shacks and saloons. It was not as busy as it had looked from the ridge outside of town, but busy enough, with drovers marching down the resounding boardwalks, singing and chaffing each other. Four of them standing drunk out in the street, singing off-key barbershop quartet.

The moon was up bright and full, now, paling the kerosene lanterns, the pitch-pine torches flaring beside the curtained crib doors. The street smelled of sagebrush and buffalo grass, beer-soaked wood, and the sweet lilac perfume of the whores. Sweet gentian and lilac.

Lacy humped the saddle and possibles along, breath coming short under the weight. Seemed like he'd hauled this baggage one damn too many miles. Too many miles—and two fist-fights too many. Getting old.

A tall, thin drover with a cast in his left eye came ducking out of a faro shack and knocked Lacy half around. "Say you!"

The drover turned, ready for a fight.

"Take it easy, Bob. I'm looking for Miss Susan Maynard's."

The drover unclenched his fists, and stood staring at Lacy, swaying a bit from side to side.

"Maynard's?" he said. "That's costly split-tail, Mister."

"Just the same. . ."

"Okay, it's up the street. All the way to the end. Last house, north side of the street. Got an empty yard, both sides."

"Much obliged," Lacy said, hoisted the saddle higher on his shoulder, and turned to go on his way.

"Mister," the drover said, "looks like you need you a horse!" and Lacy heard him stomp away up the boardwalk, his boots booming on the planking.

A horse like Talbot's gray. And that gray had to be a six—seven—hundred dollar horse, even if Talbot would sell him. There'd been a time. Well, it was a little steep, right now.

He found the house just where the drover'd said. End of the street, past the end of the street, really, with empty yards both sides of it. Likely the madam owned both parcels. It was a bigger house that most along the street. And painted white. Fresh-painted, too, shining bright in the moonlight. Gold lamplight shining out through the parlor windows. A piano tinkling along. *Just Before the Battle, Mother*, it sounded like. Civilization. And Lacy was damned glad to see it.

He pushed through the gate in the low, white picket

fence—the fence didn't do much fencing, it was just a twenty, thirty foot strip across the front yard for show—and he lugged his saddle and bedroll and rifle up the front steps onto the porch, and dropped it all with a jingle and thump beside the front door.

Someone inside must have taken that for a proper knock on the door, because Lacy heard footsteps, and then the door swung half open.

A young black girl looked out. She was dressed up like a housemaid in a black dress and white apron and cap, and she gave Lacy a careful look by light of the porch lantern.

"No cowboys here," she said.

"I'm no cowboy," Lacy said. "Now you call your mistress, pronto."

The black girl gave Lacy another look.

"We don't put up with no trouble here," she said.

"I'm not trouble, damn it. I'm a customer! Now you get your mistress, Sis, or I'll come in and get her myself!"

The black girl goggled her eyes at him, ducked back inside, and closed the door with a snap.

There was a little wait. Then the door swung open again.

The littlest old lady that Lacy had seen was standing in the doorway looking up at him.

The biggest black man that he had ever seen was standing behind her.

Lacy saw the black man wasn't armed. But in close, big as he was, he wouldn't need to be.

"What do you wish here, Mister?" the little lady said. She was tiny, and respectable-looking as any Philadelphia bluestocking. A black widow's dress, and a little lace cap with black ribbons. She had a face like a pet white monkey, shriveled and sharp. A blue-eyed little monkey.

"I want some soap and hot water for a bath, a beef-steak dinner, a soft bed for the night, and a charming young

78

lady's companionship,'' Lacy said.

The old lady thought about that, and gave Lacy another look. "You talk like a high-roller down on your luck," she said, and made to close the door.

"I'm off the trail, not off my luck," Lacy said. Then, tired and losing his temper, "Don't push yours."

The little lady stood staring at him, and the black man towering behind her looked at him as well. Then she stepped back and pulled the door wide. "Come on in, then," she said. She seemed to be a clever woman, who had seen considerable of the elephant.

Walking in, Lacy saw that the big black man, who was dressed up as a manservant in a black suit and shiny black shoes, was sweating down his shirtfront like a horse. It was strange, because the evening was cool enough, and he had no cause to be that scared of Lacy.

"You come with me," the little lady said, and led Lacy down the hall to a narrow flight of carpeted stairs. There was the noise of a party, and bright lamplight coming from a doorway to the left, but Miss Maynard sailed on by and started up the stairs.

"I have possibles on your porch," Lacy said.

The little lady turned and called back down the stairs, "William, go out and bring the gentleman's baggage upstairs." Then she turned and went on, with Lacy climbing up behind her.

The carpet on the stairs was thick as grass, soft under his boots; the house smelled of clean people. Oil lamps glowed on the gold-papered walls. From below, he could hear the piano playing some soft German music. No barrelhouse for this set-up, nothing loud or rough.

Soft and sweet was the tune this house played. A class turn-out for class johns.

# CHAPTER NINE

Miss Maynard let the way down an upstairs corridor, past a row of shut doors—Lacy heard a girl giggling—to an open door at the end of the hall.

It was a small, square room done up in the same lush style as downstairs, with gold-flowered wall-paper, a little pot-belly stove in the corner, and a big brass-pipe bed with what looked to be a fine feather mattress on it.

There was an armchair in the corner across from the stove, and Miss Maynard sat down in it, hitching herself back like a child until her tiny booted feet were swinging clear of the carpet. She stared up at Lacy, her wrinkled monkey's face screwed up with concentration. "What's your name?" she said.

"Finn Lacy. Most people just call me 'Lacy.' "

Big William came puffing into the room with Lacy's saddle and possibles. He put them on a chest at the foot of the bed, except for the rifle. He opened a tall wardrobe, and stood the scabbarded Sharps up in there. The big man was still sweating up a storm.

"All right, William," Miss Maynard said.

The black man gave Lacy a quick, cold-eyed look, top to bottom, then walked out of the room. The floor creaked under him.

When he was gone, and the door closed behind him, Miss Maynard hitched herself forward in the armchair. "You uttered a threat against me out on my porch, Mister Lacy. I take that very ill." Her pale blue eyes were as dead and still as only an old madam's come to be; her tiny face was wrinkled as a soft silk shirt.

Lacy saw no reason to be coy with her.

"You treated me rudely, Miss Maynard." He smiled at her. "I think you've been out in the high grass too long, if you can't tell a drover from a sport."

Miss Maynard contemplated him for a moment. "Who do you know, then, Mister Lacy? For I certainly have never seen you before."

"Reba Ruth, Martha Cosgrave, Many Anne Collins."

"Martha Cosgrave is dead, Mister Lacy."

"Is she really? I'll be damned. I would have said not even God would have taken on old Martha."

"Fierce, was she?" said Miss Maynard.

"Nothing like that." He got up off the bed. "Martha was a talker, Miss Maynard. She never stopped talking, but I aim to, right now."

She scooted up out of the armchair and stood to face him. She came to just above his waist. "Very well," she said, "you had Martha pegged. What are you, Mister Lacy—in the life, I mean?"

"A mack, for a while, some years back. I ran a place myself, too."

"Straight or special?"

"Straight."

"And where was that?"

Lacy threw his bed-roll onto the brass-pipe bed, untied it,

and pulled out his battered dressing-case, his soap and razor case. "You have a man in town here who can set and sharpen razors?"

Miss Maynard flushed a little, and then said, "William can do that."

"Here," Lacy handed the razor-case to her. "I'm tired of shaving with my knife." He took the thick woolen blanket up from the bedroll and threw it on the floor. "If you'll send that girl up here, I'll want that blanket cold-washed and line-dried. *Not* stove-dried. And I've got other things to be washed, too."

Miss Maynard flushed a little more. "I charge a high fee for any *hotel* service, Mister Lacy."

"When the girl's come up and got that stuff, Miss Maynard, I'll want a tin tub, soap, and buckets of hot water to go with them. Then, I'll want a beefsteak dinner with cold beer."

"Cold beer," said Miss Maynard.

"And afterward, your nicest girl. A sweet girl who likes her work, Miss Maynard. And a healthy girl, mind."

"A healthy girl," said Miss Maynard.

"And don't bother us till noon tomorrow."

"Not till noon, huh?" Miss Maynard said. "And how the fuck much do you think that'll cost you, sport?"

"I think you'll charge me twenty-five dollars in gold."

"That's right!" Miss Maynard said, and she wished she'd thought before she'd said it.

"But I'll be paying twenty," Lacy said.

Miss Maynard gritted her teeth. "And suppose I have the town marshal whip you, and throw you out of my place?" she said.

"Oh, I don't think you'll do that, dear," Lacy said.

"You don't, huh?" Miss Maynard said, ignoring the "dear."

"No, dear," Lacy said, digging gold pieces out of his purse. "Not unless you want the marshal's brains all over your wallpaper."

Miss Maynard took the twenty dollars, and left the room in a dignified fashion, looking thoughtful. Lacy went to the door after her, and called down the corridor: "If the girl's going to be hungry, then double up on that beefsteak!"

There are a few things better feeling than a bathtub full of hot water, to a butt that's sore and weary from a full day of buckboarding over the ruts of a prairie trail. A few things. And Lacy looked forward to them, too, as he soaped and soaked in the steaming water. The black girl had spread a canvas square over the carpet before setting the tub down; even so, Lacy tried not to slop over too much. Miss Maynard might forgive his bulling his way into the house; she likely wouldn't forgive a ruined carpet.

The soap the girl had given him was perfumed with lily-of-the-valley. It made a nice change from dust, sweat, and horseshit.

Big William tapped on the door, then came in. He glanced at the Bisley Colt hanging from one of the bottom bedposts beside the tub, and then stood waiting while Lacy stood in the tub and poured the last bucket of hot water over his head for a rinse. Lacy stepped out, reached to pick the towel off the chest, and started drying himself.

The big black man hauled the full tub over to the window, drew aside the curtains, raised the sash, and tilted the tub up with a grunt to pour the soapy water out into the yard below. A breath of cool night air drifted in the window.

"Leave it open," Lacy said.

The big man nodded, shouldered the empty tub, and

started out of the room.

"Hold on," Lacy said. He went to the bed, took a two-bit piece out of his purse, and handed it to the man. "Thanks for lugging that hot water up here."

The big man stared at him, nodded, and carried the tub out. He was sweating hard. It could have been the work, but Lacy thought the man looked sick.

The girl came up then, and Lacy gave her two-bits, too. She collected the canvas carpet-cover, and Lacy's blanket and dirty clothes. That left him nothing to wear but the towel; he knotted it around his waist, and went to look out the window.

A cool, starry night. He could see down part of South Street. Fewer lights, fewer people out on the street. Not much noise. On Saturday nights, Lacy supposed, the action went on until dawn. Unless this was a Saturday night. Lacy tried counting back from the time the dun had gone down under him. Had that been a Tuesday or a Thursday?

There was another tap on the door.

"Come on in."

It opened part way, and a round, freckled face looked around it.

It was a girl.

"Come in, honey."

She came sashying in, smiling. A right fresh apple tart. Fresh from some farm she looked, with her broad, pretty face, straw-yellow hair up in braids, and bright little blue eyes. Her face and arms were all dusted with freckles.

"Dinner's comin' up," she said, and swayed up to Lacy, wiggling her hips. "I'm eatin' with you. I could do a beefsteak fine." She reached down to touch him through the towel. "Do yours, for sure," she said.

"Take it easy, Little Bit," Lacy said. "You're not rushing a two-buck john. We've got all night."

She made a face at him. "All right," she said, and stood off to give him the once-over. Lacy saw that they'd dressed her up like a farm girl, too. Blue gingham dress and bare feet. She was a well-made girl. White-skinned and stocky, and strong. Her calves looked to be rounded and white under the dress. She had neat ankles, and her small feet were clean.

"What do they call you," Lacy said. "Suky-Mae?"

The girl threw back her head and laughed. She had a good, rich, easy whore's laugh, the kind of laugh that decent women never could seem to let loose. Most decent women. Lacy'd known one that laughed like a whore, but was as nice a girl as any on earth. Long time ago.

"They call me 'Silky' 'cause my skin's so soft," the girl said. "Feel." She held out a round, plump arm.

Lacy felt it. Her skin was very soft.

"What are you going to do to me?" she said to Lacy in a different-sounding deeper voice as he held her arm. "What are you going to do to me, bad man? Are you going to make me suck on your thing?"

She was good at her job. A class girl, in a class house.

"What I'm going to make you do, is pass the salt, if that damn dinner ever gets up here.

She smiled at him, not fooled. "You been around," she said. "But that don't make any difference."

And she was right. Mack or high-roller, when it came to cock-and-cunt, the cunt whistled the tune right along.

"Come here."

She came closer to him, and Lacy reached out and took her by the shoulders and turned her around. Then he bent down and breathed softly on the back of her neck, ruffling the soft tendrils of yellow hair. He waited a long moment, then he put his mouth on the tender back of her neck and bit, first softly, then not so softly.

She didn't move; she stood still as he nuzzled into her neck, biting. When he took his mouth away, he saw goose-bumps down the soft white skin of her upper arm. It was a stroke of luck, or a deliberate move by Miss Maynard, to see that he got a girl who liked it, rather than one with a girl friend, or one that didn't give a damn.

Lacy turned her back around to face him. "What's Miss Maynard want to know?" he said.

The girl looked up at him for a moment, then sighed. "She wants to know who you are, where you come from, what you're doin' in town."

Lacy smiled. "Well, I'll tell you; then we won't have to worry about it. My name's Lacy. It's not my real name." The girl made a comic face and rolled her eyes. "That's new," she said. "And," Lacy said, "I come from north of here. And I'm only staying in this town till I can rest up, buy me a horse, and get the hell out! Now, do you think Lady Tom Thumb'll be satisfied with that?"

"*What* did you call her?" the girl said. "*Lady Tom Thumb*?" She rolled out that rich laugh again. "Oh, the girls'll love that one. They'll love it!"

There was a tap on the door, and the black girl came in carrying a big wooden tray. "Here's your dinner, folks," she said. "Exceptin' you don't get no potatoes, Miz Silky. Miz Maynard's orders 'cause you get too fat."

Silky pouted a little at that. "You can have half mine," Lacy said, and she eased up.

The black girl put the tray down on the chest at the foot of the bed. "Y'all don't have no table in here."

"That's all right. What's your name?"

"Sarah," she said.

"Thanks, Sarah. I've been causing you some work, tonight, I guess."

"Why, that's all right," the girl said, "Doin' for folks is

what I get paid for." She lingered by the tray, arranging the platters on it.

"Sarah," Silky said, "didn't he already give you a tip?"

"Well, I think so," Sarah said.

"Then stop foolin' with that dinner and get your black ass out of here, 'cause he ain't goin' to tip you twice!"

Sarah stuck out her tongue at Silky, and then hustled out and shut the door.

"She's nice, but she's awful greedy," Silky said.

"Nothing worse that a greedy girl," Lacy said, dragging the armchair up to the chest for her.

Silky laughed, and took the covers off the plates. "Golly," she said "rib-eye steaks! I guess the one with the potatoes is yours."

Lacy sat down on the foot of the bed. "Will you just take those damn potatoes?"

"I don't want 'em all!"

She left him one piece.


"Set the tray outside the door," Lacy said, "and come on to bed." He blew out the standing oil lamps, then bent and blew out the one beside the bed. The room flooded with moonlight. He picked his gunbelt off the bottom bedpost, and hung it over the bedpost at the head of the bed, the one near the window. Then he took the towel off, pulled back the bed covers, and slid in between the sheets.

The coolness, the smoothness, were so sweet that he groaned aloud. It felt like floating in cool water.

Silky stood at the other end of the bed, and tugged her dress over her head. She was naked under it. Her body shone like milk in the moonlight.

He watched her as she folded her dress and moved through the moonlight to put it on the chest at the foot of the bed. Her breasts moved as she walked. She had a neat, round butt, like a pony's.

"Damn it," she said, coming back to her side of the bed, "Where's the pot? I got to pee. That beer just runs right through me." And she ducked down out of sight to search under the bed for it.

Lacy lay in the coolness of the bed, listening to the distant sounds down the street as the last drovers sang to the moon, to the German piano music rising faintly up the stairs. It was a very quiet crowd at Miss Maynard's.

There was a sudden, bright, continuous musical note across the bed.

Silky had found the pot.

# CHAPTER TEN

She rolled into Lacy's arms as white, as smooth and sweet as whipped cream. But heavy cream, solid with muscle in her arms and thighs and ass, soft and smooth in her breasts and belly. He turned her onto one of the pillows, so her face was full in the bright moonlight from the window. Her blue eyes were black in the moonlight.

"What are you going to do to me?" she whispered to him.

Lacy gathered her full, fat breasts in his hands, squeezing them gently, and he bent his head to suck at her nipples. She sighed, and turned her head on the pillow, her eyes closed against the light. Her straw-yellow hair was coming down, long, curling strands of it falling across her white throat.

Lacy grazed on her, as a stud horse might graze on a green meadow, his mouth drifting down from her breasts to the curve of her ribs, the gleaming, soft skin of her belly. He nipped at the tender skin, and tongued her navel.

"Ummm. . ." She purred, and he felt her fingers tangle in his hair.

He threw the covers back all the way, reached down and gripped her behind the knees, and gently lifted, doubling her legs up until her knees almost touched her breasts.

Her blond-furred cunt, her spraddled ass-cheeks were up, presented to him—and he bent and drove his mouth into her.

He ate into her as if he were starving. Licking and biting at her cunt, opening it up, spreading it wet and glistening under his tongue. She tasted bitter-sweet.

"Oh, Jesus! You *are* a bad man."

Lacy used all his old mack tricks on her, wanting, the way he always wanted, to make her change, become different from what she had been when he took her to bed. He worked at her, and he spread her wider and licked the crease of her ass.

"Oh. . .oh!" She heaved under his mouth, the smooth, strong thighs thrashing, clamping to hold him there. He thrust his tongue straight into her, searching with the tip of it through the wet folds. He pushed into her hard, almost roughly, prodding into her, moving his face from side to side.

She made a humming sound in her throat and suddenly tried to twist away from him, to get away from what he was doing to her.

Lacy held her hard. He dug his fingers into her thighs, and held her to his mouth. He held her down on the bed as if he were killing her.

She kicked, bucking under him as he licked and sucked at her. A starving man at a French dinner.

"Oh—don't!" She struggled against him for a moment more. "Oooh. . . ow, ow!" She shouted, and he felt the muscles in her round thighs stiffen. She shoved her wet cunt up hard into his face, shoving it up at him. He felt her opening wider, wetter, under his tongue. She tasted like

90

salt, and as he licked at her, he felt her grow slippery fat and swollen. Full, and oily, and tight. Wet and puffed with coming.

Golly!'' Lacy felt her slowly relax against him. ''Oh, golly. . . what a sport you are. . .''

His cock was so hard it hurt him.

He slid up onto her, and she hugged him hard, feeling his hard cock. ''No, no. . . not yet. I couldn't.''

''I know,'' Lacy said, biting her ear gently, kissing it. ''I know. But soon you will.''

Silky turned her head to kiss him on the mouth. Staring up at him with moon-black eyes. She giggled. ''You gam me finer than a girl,'' she said. ''Where did you learn how a woman's made?''

''I macked for a while.''

''Oh, lord, I should have known it.'' She reached down to rub her thighs. ''You hurt me, holding me so hard like that.'' She giggled again. ''I thought you were going to bite me down there. Eat me up!''

''Maybe I will, next time,'' Lacy said.

''You pimps are all alike,'' she said. ''You hurt a poor girl to hold her.'' She put her hands up to Lacy's face, and brought him down to kiss her. Then she sighed and turned to nestle in his arms.

''But you're out of the life, now?''

''Yes. For a long time.''

''Ah, God. . . I'd like to get out of it myself, if I didn't like the money and the fuckin'.'' She started to laugh, and Lacy laughed, too.

''It's just that that holds you, is it?''

''Wasn't for the money and the fuckin', I'd be out of it in a shot.'' And she started laughing again, her breasts shaking. Her teeth shining in the moonlight.

She hugged him, and said, ''And why did you get out,

Sport? Did you find something better to do?''

*Something better to do.* . .Found himself doing something better, was more like it. Drawing a pistol and killing better than most men could. That was something better. A man can run a whorehouse, even two of them, and be known as a rough customer—indeed, had better been known as a hard-case, if he wants to keep some cadet from stealing his business.

But kill two men in a gunfight. And then another three men before the year was out? That had been a little too ripe, even for Fort Smith. In that situation, a smart young man sells out his fixed assets and gets out of town.

And never stopped getting out of town, after that, one way and another.

Still getting out of town, maybe. . .

''I liked moving around,'' he stroked the girl's stomach. ''I didn't like sitting in one place.''

''Not even countin' cash 'n' gash, huh?''

''Not even with that.''

''Men are fools,'' Silky said, and she reached down between them to grip his cock. ''Tell me what to do,'' she said.

''Get your mouth on it,'' Lacy said. ''See if I let you suck out some jizz.''

She turned on her hands and knees in the moonlight, the smooth long lines of her back shining like snow, and took his cock in her hands. It was swollen hard, and aching.

''Does it hurt you?'' she said. She stroked it gently, squeezing it. Lacy heard her breathing. Then she dipped her head, and he felt the cool wet of her tongue as she lapped at the head of his cock.

''Some is coming out, already,'' she said, and bent her head to lick at it again. She put her lips on it and sucked it.

Then she stopped and took a breath, and lowered her

head again to lick at him like a cat. Licking up the length of his cock, her head moving like a cat's cleaning itself. He felt the night air cool on him as she wet him with her tongue. She ducked her head lower and nuzzled at his balls, breathing hard through her nose as she sucked and licked at him.

Lacy felt the pleasure coming.

He reached down to run his fingers through her hair, to grip her gently, and hold her still.

"Another time for that way; another time for your mouth," he said. "I want to finish up in you."

She turned on her hands and knees again, up to the head of the bed, and put her head down into the pillow, her round white ass thrust up into the air.

Lacy could smell her, now, a warm, salty smell. Fish blood.

He got up behind her, lifted her thighs and spread them. Then he put up his hand, and the girl groaned as he felt her. Hot, slippery wetness, and the soaked curls below it. He put his thumb into her. The wetness made sounds.

He took his swollen cock in his hand, and nudged the head of it against her, feeling the heat, the rough wet curls, then the heat again. He rubbed the head of his cock up and down into her, and felt her ass move back, moving back into him as he did it.

He put the head to her, and just into her.

Then he slowly drove in all the way.


She was tight, for a whore. Tight, and oily with juice. And warm as cooked meat. He seemed to go into her forever.

She moaned into the pillow, and he pressed hard against her ass, feeling the smooth full cheeks cool against him, the hot, squeezing grip of her cunt holding him in her.

Then he slowly pulled out, looking down, watching his cock, glistening with her juice, slowly pulling out of the wet shadow of her cunt, shining with her juice in the moonlight.

When he was almost out of her, she moved her ass to hold him, murmuring into the pillow. Lacy gripped her with one hand at the nape of her neck, slid his other hand under her to pull gently at her nipples, and began to fuck her.

He took his time. And he was gentle with her.

He rode his cock into her all the way, and felt the slippery touch of her womb at the tip. And out—and in her again. It made wet noises, each time. The girl was groaning into the pillow, her fists clenched beside her head.

Lacy moved a little harder, a little faster.

Her ass moved against him, thrusting back against him each time he went into her.

He bowed his back and drove into her hard. Ramming it deep into her, feeling the pleasure rising like a tide in his belly. "Oh, Christ!" He gritted his teeth.

The girl beneath him was writhing now, her round white ass moving frantically, impaled on the wet pole of his cock. A rapid wet sound as he fucked into her.

The girl squealed suddenly, bucking on the bed like a pony. She moaned "Mama," into the pillow—and Lacy let it come.

He groaned and jerked as it pumped out of him. A pleasure so great that it hurt him, throbbing, flooding out of him into her. He fell forward over her, hugging her to him as his cock jerked in her. He felt her cunt swollen, hot and slippery with her spending.

Then he rolled over onto his side, still holding her, hugging her, her breasts in his hands.

They lay a while like that, the moonlight shining down

on them through the tall window, the night air cool on their skin. Lacy buried his face in her hair, breathing in the sweet smell of it. Soap, and perfume, and girl-sweet.

Not many better times than this. . .

He felt his muscles uncoil and ease. And he lay content, her smooth, soft, round weight in his arms.

She turned to him after a while, and snuggled back into his arms, and he reached down and tugged the covers up over them. Way in the distance, a mile or so out of town, a coyote was singing to the moon, its thin, yipping wail echoing faintly over the town.

A rooster, wakened before dawn, answered him from some backyard far down the street.

Not many better times than this. . .

Lacy slept, and dreamed of mountains, and a gray horse.


He woke with the noontime sun flooding in through the window. The other side of the bed was empty; the girl was up and gone.

He yawned and stretched hard under the fine, smooth sheets, then relaxed and settled back into the soft mattress, looking out through the window at the bright dazzle of sunlight, the milk-blue sky beyond it.

Lacy felt better than he had felt in some time. Not just rested, and fed, and screwed-out, but feeling better about being alive. Better than he had felt since he rode out of Idaho.

Better than he'd felt since he'd left a girl crying, lying on the cobbles of a stable-yard. Felt good enough to be thinking he might damn well steal that lawyer's gray horse. He'd dreamed about that big gelding. Any Indian could tell you what that meant. It meant you were going to *have* that animal; if you had the gumption to steal it.

And damned if he might not do it, too! He'd never yet stolen a horse. Be a shame to miss doing that. Be a shame to ride down to Mexico on some galled-out cow-pony. And that would be about all he could buy, because he had eighty-seven dollars left over from that sweet night with a tub of hot water, a beef-steak dinner. . . and Silky.

Eighty-seven dollars would buy him some beef jerky, another box of .45's, some flour and salt, a couple of cans of tomatoes and peaches, and some real old galled-out and run-down cow-pony.

And it would be a shame, too. Riding down to Sonora to see the Don again, a fine horse was a damn-near necessity. Mexicans didn't mind a man's clothes being worn, but they sure as hell judged him a dead loss if he rode a poor horse.

It would mean coming to the Don like a man needing a favor, *needing* work. Instead of as a free *pistolero* on a thoroughbred horse, willing, perhaps, to do the Don a favor, for old time's sake.

Damn if he wasn't talking himself into it. Serve him right if he ended strung up by a bunch of cowtown rubes. Holliday would wake up in his grave and laugh.

There was a tap on the door.

Lacy hitched over nearer the bedpost where the Colt was hanging, and called out, "Come in."

Silky the farm girl came pushing in the door with a big breakfast tray in her hands. She was barefooted, and wearing a red house-coat with yellow flowers on it. She looked like a farm girl for sure this morning, her yellow hair in pigtails, her round, pretty face scrubbed and beaming.

"Ham 'n' eggs," she said, nudging the door shut with her elbow. "And fried potatoes, too."

"You can have all mine, Honey," Lacy said, hitching himself up in bed.

"I got my own, this mornin'; the old lady was lookin'

after William. He's sick." She handed the tray to Lacy, climbed into bed beside him, and then pulled the tray half onto her lap. "This side's mine. I'm just havin' three eggs."

"I thought that colored man looked bad last night." Lacy cut a bite of ham; Silky had served him up about a pound of meat, four eggs, and a considerable heap of fried potatoes. "What ails him?"

"Malaria, Miss Maynard says. He caught it in Louisiana a long time ago." Silky swallowed a bite, and forked in another. When that went down, she glanced at Lacy and said, "They're sayin' downstairs that you're a *real* badman. A famous one, now."

Lacy slowly turned his head and stared at her, his eyes like gray ice.

"What's the matter?" the girl said. Her face went pale. "What's the matter?"

# CHAPTER ELEVEN

"What do you mean, *a famous badman*?"

"I didn't mean anything!" She put her fork down on her plate with a nervous rattle. "The girls. . . the girls are just saying that downstairs, because Mrs. McCaslin at the store told Sarah you beat up Abe Bothwell." She cleared her throat. "A cowboy told her that a man named Lacy beat him up."

"Well," Lacy said, and he made himself smile, "I did have a fight with Bothwell. I sure wouldn't say I beat him up, though." He leaned over and kissed her on the cheek. "I just don't like folks talking behind my back. People have gotten into trouble, getting talked up as badmen and that sort of thing."

"Well, I wouldn't say anything," Silky said, and leaned over to return the kiss, then wiped off the bit of egg she'd left on his cheek. "I wouldn't say anything to hurt you."

"Let's eat up, then; breakfast's getting cold."

Silky chewed through her eggs and ham, leaving her potatoes for last. She sat back on the pillows to rest for a moment before tackling them, and took a swallow of coffee.

"Sarah said Miss Maynard said this breakfast is free for you. She wants to talk to you this morning before you go, she said." She sipped some more coffee, then dug into the potatoes.

"Want *my* potatoes?"

She shook her head, her mouth full. When she swallowed, she said, "I know I'm an awful pig, but I sure don't want to get as fat as Mary Withers. You'll see. Mary's damned near fat enough for a fair." She giggled. "Half the time, the men pokin' her can't even find it!" She sighed, and went back at the potatoes.

Lacy finished his breakfast, and it was a good one, but the shine was off the morning, just a touch.

*A real badman*.

Too damn close for comfort. A couple more fights, a little more trouble in this section, and it would be more than a few whores talking. More trouble, and the law would start sending telegrams out to Amarillo. And from there, maybe Montana, maybe Idaho.

It wouldn't take a really curious marshal too long to start hearing stories about a "Lee," or "Lea." Or Lacy.

"What's the best livery in town, honey? Place where I might find a decent horse to buy."

Silky was scraping her plate. "Mister Manstein runs the best livery, I guess. He's a Dutchy, and he keeps his stables real clean, too."

There was a tap on the door. Lacy glanced up at his holstered Colt, and called to whoever it was to come in.

Sarah stuck her head in the door. "Miz Maynard'd like to see you downstairs in the parlor, Mister." Then she shut the door again.

Silky got up, took the tray, and set it down on the chest at the foot of the bed. "Did you see how quick that nigger scooted? Just so she wouldn't have to carry this tray down to the kitchen. Well, I'm damned if *I* will!'' She came back to the bed, jumped in under the covers, and snuggled up to Lacy. ''We had a good time last night, didn't we?''

''One of the best, Little Bit.''

She bit him on the ear. ''I wish we could now.''

''Can't we?'' Lacy pulled her down into his lap and kissed her, tasting her mouth, rich with traces of her breakfast. She kissed him back for a moment, then pulled away.

''Miss Maynard'd charge you,'' she said. She sat up on her side of the bed, and Lacy saw that there were tears in her eyes. ''This whorin's not always so fine,'' she said. She turned and kissed him on the cheek; then she got up and went out of the room.

While Lacy was dressing, Sarah tapped at the door, and came in for the tray. She looked resentful, and gave a loud grunt as she picked it up. ''I be back with your hot water,'' she said. ''And William sharpened up your razors for you last night, before he had to lie down on his bed—he got so sick.'' She elbowed her way out the door with the tray.

Lacy left his shirt off, since he'd be shaving. No use getting wet soap on it. He stood at the window for a while, watching the wagons and horsemen, and a few women, strolling in pairs, moving up and down South Street. He could see a saddlery shop down the way, and considered buying a length of rawhide tie for lashing. Be good to have on a long ride.

Sarah tapped and came in again, with his razor case and a can of hot water. ''The blanket and clothes ain't dry yet,'' she said. She sighed.

Lacy did some sighing himself, dug two bits out of his pocket, and handed it over.

When he came downstairs, Lacy saw two girls in the hall. A tall, pretty brunette with a lot of rouge on her face, and a very fat girl with her brown hair done up high on her head. They were both in dressing gowns, and were standing in the handsome hallway arguing in bitter whispers. Most whorehouses were quiet enough during the day, when people were trying to get some sleep, to rest up from the night before, and get ready for the one coming up. But this was the first time Lacy had seen whores arguing in whispers. It wasn't the usual style. Miss Maynard ran a taut ship.

The girls saw him, stopped whispering at each other, and gave him the once-over. Lacy supposed the fat one was Mary Withers.

Lacy walked from the bottom of the staircase up the front hall to the parlor, hearing the girls begin to whisper again behind him. A very quiet house.

Miss Maynard was sitting in the front parlor, waiting for him. She was perched in a rocking chair, her feet well off the floor, sewing at a sampler.

"Good morning, Mister Lacy." She set her sewing down on a small table beside the rocker. "Sit down, please; make yourself comfortable." She nodded at an armchair.

Lacy sat. "Thanks for the breakfast," he said. He wondered what the old lady wanted. Miss Maynard didn't seem the sort to give anything away. Even breakfasts.

"I do hope," the old lady said, looking Lacy over with her dead blue eyes. "I do hope you spent a pleasant evening with our Miss Perkins."

*Silky* Perkins.

"Miss Perkins is a charmer," Lacy said, "and very lady-like." He thought that would please Miss Maynard, and he was right. The wrinkled little white-capped head bobbed in approval. "I would not board a girl who wasn't," she said. "I will not have a girl who has to be whipped. A bad-behaved girl can spoil an entire house."

"Damned right," Lacy said. "What can I do for you, Miss Maynard?"

It seemed she thought he was a mite abrupt; her monkey face screwed into a sudden frown, but it smoothed out as she rocked slowly back and forth, extending one tiny foot at each forward rock, to touch a brocaded foot-stool and rock her back again.

"My William is sick," she said. "The malaria. He caught it in Louisiana."

"That so?"

She stopped rocking. "I understand that you are a hard-case, Mister Lacy. Certainly if you punished Abraham Both-well, you must be." She glanced at Lacy's Colt. "At least with your fists. And that is all that I require."

Lacy tried to keep his face straight, but he couldn't; he knew he was smiling at her. "Are you asking me to play bouncer for you, Miss Maynard?"

She gave him a colder than usual look. "You are both a slighter man, and an older man, than I would usually employ as a doorman here." That to put him in his place. "And in any case, *bouncing* is in no way required. My clients here are gentlemen—and they behave like gentlemen—or they never return. What I require—especially for the next few days, when the spring round-ups are finished—is a man to prevent intruders, cowboys, if you wish, from entering and disturbing the house."

She settled back and started rocking again.

"What would you pay?" Lacy said.

"Ten dollars a night, and room and board out back."

Lacy sat back in the armchair and thought about it. Private fights were one thing, range fights the same. That could draw the law on him fast enough—and though there were no warrants out for him in Texas, not even old ones—that would be only the beginning of trouble.

Bouncing in a whorehouse was a different matter. It would pin him as a common brawler, a brawler at the service of the peace, at that. The peace of the town's "gentlemen," at their pleasures.

But the money wasn't enough. Not enough to keep him in Bristolton for the next week. Not enough for the gray horse, either.

"No," he said, "not on those terms."

Miss Maynard stopped rocking. Probably regretting the free breakfast.

"I will do that job for you, though," he said. "And for free, for nothing." Miss Maynard looked disturbed. She was a very old little lady, and had learned that nothing was free.

"I'll keep your door for you—as long as I can sit in on any poker game in the house."

Miss Maynard looked as though she couldn't believe her ears. "You mean to sharp my clients?"

"No," Lacy said, shaking his head. "I'd play dead square. And you could tell your customers that I was a professional, too."

"And have you take my clients to the laundry? I think not!"

"That I wouldn't do. If I lose, I lose. But I won't play to win more than a few hundred from any john, and if the total runs over a thousand for the week, I'll give it to the house."

Miss Maynard paused to think about that.

"It might add a nice edge to your business. To have a fast, but straight game of poker going on in the house. Truth is, a lot of johns aren't as interested in fucking as they like to make out."

"That's true. That's true," she said. "And they do play sometimes, anyway."

"If any customer objects, I don't sit in. Keeps everything friendly, that way."

"And how do I know you'd play straight?"

"Not worth it to mark the deck for a few hundred. And everything over a thousand goes to you, anyway. I'm sure as hell not marking a deck for you, Miss Maynard."

Miss Maynard rocked a little faster, thinking.

"It would be just for the next few days," she said. "Just till William's back on his feet again."

"That's right. I'm not interested in staying in town; I just want a stake to travel."

"It could mean trouble, just the same," she said. "Business is fine as it is."

"You'd just be trying the game for a week, and likely making some money at it. If turns out to work well, then you could get another dealer in when I'm gone. Make a regular thing of it."

The old lady picked up her sampler, and started working on it, rocking gently, as if Lacy had left the room. Her wrinkled lips were pursed. She set three or four slow stitches.

"We'll try it tonight," she said. "Just for tonight. If my people like the game. . . well, then we'll see." She looked up at him. "My customers are important people, Mister Lacy. They may make fools of themselves over a stupid girl's cunny; but otherwise they're right smart. They wouldn't like it—and I wouldn't like it—if you should be trying some sort of scammer here. I mean," she lifted her sampler to her mouth and neatly bit off her thread, "that they would have your legs broken—or I would."

Lacy smiled and stood up. "I have some business in town. I'll be back before dark to start work." He stopped smiling.

"We have a deal, Miss Maynard."

The old lady nodded. "For tonight," she said.

Lacy walked down the corridor through the house, and then the kitchen. Three of the girls were sitting at the kitchen table having coffee; one of them was the tall brunette who'd been arguing with the fat girl in the hallway.

"Morning, girls."

The brunette nodded. The other two, thin brown-eyed girls who looked to have some Mexican blood, just stared at him.

Lacy went on out the back door, and down the steps into the yard. There was a kitchen garden laid out there, and the outhouse looked like a fine four-holer. No real fence around the yard, except for a two-strand wire fence around the garden to keep town stock from wandering in.

It was clear all the way out to the brush at the edge of town. A straight run down the hall, through the kitchen, and out. Lacy was alive because he'd always scouted the back way out. Most particularly the back way out of saloons and whorehouses.

Going back to cards. . . That was a comedown for such a reformed character. Not one damn game of poker played in more than four years. Not one whore marketed, either, not for a lot more than four years.

And no man killed for money—or for pleasure either. A few, in the last years, for necessity. Bitter necessity. None for money. None for pleasure.

But dealing poker in a whorehouse was cutting it fine. She would have hated to see him doing this again.

He walked to the outhouse, opened a door and went in. The closet was clean and whitewashed, with a neat stack of cleaning paper stuck on a nail by the seat.

A class house.


Lacy walked up South Street, past a row of sheds and stockyards, and then crossed the street to the saddlery. Town looked busy in the afternoon; the street was full of drays and wagons, hauling ranch-goods, mostly, posts, and feeders, wire, salt blocks, and trimmed lumber. Lot of people on the boardwalks, cowpokers and loafers, some clerks and Irish laborers. Not many women shopping on South Street. Whores just getting out of bed; ladies staying north of the line.

There were a lot of fice dogs in town, running up and down the street, yapping at the horses. No kids, though; firm in the schoolhouse, the poor little bastards.

The sun, slanting into deep afternoon, still came striking bright and hot, bouncing off the light gray, weathered boards all the buildings were made of.

Texas spring.

The saddlery shop was dark and cool. A bell nailed to the door jingled when Lacy pushed the door shut behind him.

"I'll be go to hell," a deep voice said. "If it ain't Buckskin Frank Leslie, in the flesh."

Lacy drew and turned to kill the man that was talking.

# CHAPTER TWELVE

A face as pale as paper stared at him through the shadows. Pale face over black beard, behind a low counter.

Lacy centered the face as he finished turning, squeezing the trigger to put the round into the forehead.

And eased up, fast.

Lacy heard the sounds of the world rush back, and the motions of the world, too, as he lifted the Colt's muzzle and began to lower the hammer.

"Oh, for Christ's sake don't kill me, Frank!" The pale face worked, a long way behind Lacy's draw, and decision not to shoot.

"Calm yourself yourself, Jeff; I won't shoot you." Lacy holstered the Colt.

*No-legs Jeff Compton.*

Silver City. Long time ago. Seven years. . .eight? Lost both legs to some accident. . . a mine tram. Went to working leather for a living. A married man.

"How's Virginia, Jeff?" Calm him a little more, he looks scared enough to be sick from it.

"What? What, Frank?"

"Virginia."

"Oh. . .oh." Compton cleared his throat and put his hands down carefully on the counter. There were fine braided belts laid out there, and purses with designs cut into the leather, and a handsome pair of saddlebags with elkheads cut into the shining leather of the flaps. Good work.

"Virginia's dead, Frank. Got a pain in her belly and died of it. In Colorado."

"I'm sorry to hear that, Jeff; she was a considerable woman."

"Yes," Compton said. "Yes, she was." Lacy saw the gray in Compton's beard; his eyes had adjusted to the dimness of the shop. There was a fly buzzing around the window, trying to get out into the sunshine.

"Sorry I drew on you, Jeff. I don't use that name, anymore. I don't want to be called it, either."

"I see," Compton cleared his throat again. "I guess I just didn't think. I saw you come in the shop, and I recognized you right away. You changed all right, but I just recognized you right away. . ."

"No harm done, Jeff." Lacy thought of coming to the shop—Compton certainly lived in the room behind it—coming to it late tonight, and killing the man. He thought about it, and perhaps something showed in his face.

"I swear to you, Fr—. I swear I'll not say a single word you don't want." Compton looked down at the counter, at his hands. "You can't kill everybody who cuts your trail. Not a man with no legs, who never hurt anybody."

"My name's Finn Lacy now, Jeff."

"Okay. Okay, Mister Lacy. I won't forget it, either."

"You don't, Jeff, and I'll consider it a personal favor. You *do* forget, and I would consider that a deliberate injury done to me."

108

"You don't have to worry about that, Mister Lacy."

"Just Lacy."

Compton nodded. He took his hands off the counter, and wiped them on his shirt.

Lacy leaned over the counter and held out his hand. "How's it been going for you, Jeff? It's good to see a familiar face."

Compton shook Lacy's hand, smiling with relief. He had a powerful grip from years of wheeling his bath chair. "You ornery old son-of-a-bitch," he said. "You like to scared the shit right out of me!"

"You gave me a jump, too," Lacy said.

"You know that's the first time I actual saw you draw?" He shook his head. "Man, you're the fastest pull I ever saw!"

"Not what I was."

"If you were ever quicker than that, I don't believe it."

He wheeled the chair out from behind the counter, his big shoulders heaving as he shoved on the wheel rims. He planted himself in the center of the small shop floor, and looked Lacy up and down.

"Older, by God. . . Lacy. Older, and some gray in your hair, too. And scarred-up like an old range bull!" He shook his head. "These damn years are ruining us!"

"Yes, they are," Lacy said.

"Remember Bud Philpot?"

"Bank robber."

Compton snorted. "So he'd say. Robbed one damn mine camp bank—and dead drunk at the time. Started cryin' when he woke up and found he'd really done it!"

Lacy shrugged. "And spent the money on that pretty sissy. . . Jason. . .something. Boys called him Jassie."

"That's it. Well, that boy *was* better lookin' than any woman in a hundred miles, unless you went into Silver for a spree." He leaned at ease in the wicker chair. "Well sir, that fool Philpot was at Landru's one day, and a bunch of us was sittin' around, talkin' about some crazy old coot prospectin' the Sawtooths—and Philpot speaks right up an' says: 'Not for me—no sirree! I don't want to get old! Death come quick, and catch me young an' good-lookin'!'"

"I can just hear him."

"You ought to have! You were gone out of the mountains by then, and you missed it. For sure as I'm sittin' here in this god-damned chair, Philpot was caught at Swede's camp the *very next day*—caught and et alive by a grizzly bear!"

"No shit."

"No shit! The very next day!"

"He shouldn't have talked trash in those mountains."

Compton nodded thoughtful. "You know, that's right. Stuff a man can get away with on the flat, he shouldn't ought to try it on in high country. Too close to the real spooks, up there."

"Well." He spun the chair, "Here I am yarnin' away on your butt, and I guess you came in here to buy somethin'—before you damn near shot my head off, *Mister Lacy*." He wheeled himself back in behind the counter. "What can I do you for?"

"I came in for some rawhide ties."

"Now, hell, wouldn't you know it? I do the best damn leatherwork in North Texas, and all you want is some old scrap ties?" He bent to dig into a bin beneath the counter.

"You know," he said, his voice muffled as he rummaged, "I've got a pistol down here just for trouble-some owlhooters like you." He came up puffing, and hitched back in his chair with a grunt. He held out a bundle of rawhide cord.

"Go on, take what you want. I don't use the shit."

Lacy took the bundle and started sorting the strips out.

"I've got this damn pistol under the counter," Compton said. "Always figured if any hardcase came in to rob me, why I'd show up like Bill Hickok!" He laughed. "And just now when it looked like it was really *happenin'*, well, I was scared to death."

"Jeff," Lacy said. "Shooting people is nothing special; Damn fools do it every day. It's no great gift to be given, to be able to do that." He wound up a coil of three rawhide strips, and handed the rest of the bundle back. "This is all I need." He thought a minute, looking at the tooled saddlebags. It was fine work. Look pretty on that damn gray.

"Tell you what you can do, if you will."

"Name it," Compton said.

"Set those saddlebags aside for a few days. Could be I'll have the cash for them then. That's handsome work."

"I'll hold 'em for you."

"What's the price?"

"Let me see, now. Well—"

"Full price, Jeff."

"Eight dollars too steep?"

"Done. And if I make the cash, I'll want you to do me up a buckskin vest, too. I'll call in, let you know in a day or two. Mine's getting too smoky to wear."

"Buckskin?" Compton said.

"Why not?" Lacy said, smiling.


Lacy strolled up the side street torward Main. Jeff Compton had said Silky was right about Manstein being the town's best livery-man. May as well have a look-in at those horses. Jeff had also described the marshal. Man named Charles Clay. Lacy had never heard of him.

"Wouldn't be likely to see him, either," Jeff had said. "Friend to the big money, enemy to the small."

And out of town, too, more often than not. Probably reining out of the cattle company's way. "Always goin' off to Amarillo to talk to the sheriff," Jeff had said. "Probably figurin' how they're goin' to stock the ranches those Company people are goin' to give 'em!"

Clay have any reputation with a gun?

" 'Bout like I do," Compton had said with a snort. "Has some big deputies go around smackin' cowboys on Saturday night, that's all. Big law around here is the town committee. Kind of a vigilance committee, but they don't like to call it that. Anybody steals a horse or back-shoots a man in this town better sprout wings and fly. Only chance he's got."

It had all sounded familiar to Lacy, and as he walked up to Main Street—the kids were loose from the school-house, now, and running around the streets raising hell, girls as well as boys—he realized why.

Bristolton was an old-fashioned town. An old-timey hard-nose cowtown, not wrung-out yet by the railroads, and the eastern banks, and English dukes with a lot of gold to throw around.

The last of its kind. One of them.

In a few years, ten, maybe fifteen at most, Bristolton will have dried up and blown away. Or the railroad will come through, and the town settles down to dullness and good behavior. Either way, it wouldn't stay the same. Probably had so far because of the Comanches. They'd held these Staked Plains for a long time. Kept the town lively, Lacy supposed. On the jump.

Kept the railroad out, too. And the big money from back east.

Well, the Commanch were broken. And in a way, Bristolton would break with them. People wouldn't be calling it *Pistoltown* much longer. . .

Main street was busy, full of traffic. Lacy wove his way along the boardwalk, heading east, toward the long, whitewashed *Livery* sign he saw two blocks away. Herbert Manstein, Jeff Compton had said, was hard but fair.

Lacy had known a lot of livery men. Liars to a man, and never fair, not unless they were dumb enough to have to make their living feeding watered oats and sandy hay to board horses. Manstein might be an exception, if he was a religious man.

Poor Jeff had no need for a horse, except for an old buggy plug. Manstein would have had no reason to sting him on a trade.

A pretty girl, hand in hand with a little boy, blocked Lacy's way for a moment. The three of them did the this-way-duck and the that-way-dodge, to try and get out of each other's way, and finally, Lacy just stood stock still, smiled, and tipped his hat till the girl scurried around him, towing the kid behind her.

"Now, there's a pretty piece of skirt."

A merry voice, just behind him.

Abe Bothwell.

Lacy turned slowly. . .no hurry at all. . .keeping his hand clear of his gun. Bothwell was standing just behind him, leaning casually against a peeled pine post holding up the awning of a dry goods store. The gun-man was smiling, his arms crossed his chest.

"No need to be itchin', Scarface. I don't need to shoot any man in the back. I will say, though, I took you for too downy a bird to be stickin' to a town where you were certain sure to be seein' me again."

Bothwell's nose was still badly swollen and discolored across the bridge. There was otherwise no sign of the fight on him.

113

Lacy noticed that other people passing by on the boardwalk were giving them plenty of room. They knew Bothwell, and were afraid of what might happen.

"We had our fight, Bothwell," Lacy said. "It was fair enough. I'll shake hands on that, if you're willing." Bothwell seemed a changeable man; it was worth a try to dodge the trouble.

Abe threw back his head and laughed. "Damned if you don't tempt me," he said. "I have a strong notion you're a nasty rascal yourself, Scarface." He sighed, and shook his head. "But I guess not. Weighin' it all up, one way and another, I believe I'd rather kill you. And the time's comin' quick when I'll be let do just that."

He winked at Lacy as if they were old friends, straightened up from the awning post, and strolled off down the boardwalk steps and out across the street. He didn't look back. He carried those two big Remington .44's well.

Lacy stood looking after him. Considering the usefulness of calling Bothwell right there. Probably not worth the trouble. And there was always the chance a man like Bothwell might, after all, be quick enough to put him down. Not much chance. But some.

One thing he'd seen. Bothwell did cross-draw instead of turning his wrist to draw those reversed guns with his same-side hands. Abe had spilled the beans on that when he stood at ease, with his arms crossed across his chest. Set with a small head start, if he needed it.

Let it go. Let it go. A good chance he could win some money and be out of town before Bothwell was cut loose from his leash. A good enough chance.

Lacy turned to walk on down the boardwalk toward the livery and saw Louis Bothwell standing in the shaded doorway of the dry goods store. The fat man stood in the door way like a stump, looking at Lacy without much curiosity; his dark red beard had been neatly trimmed. The black parrot-beak butt of his .38 jutted up out of his belt to lie close along his swollen gut.

Been in there all along, of course. Watching Lacy watch his brother.

If Lacy *had* called Abe, fat Louis would have broken his back for him with a bullet.

And have served him right for being so foolish as to forget Louis sitting his roan out by the Angle Iron fence. Sitting, and watching.

If it came to shooting, Lacy would somehow have to put Louis down first. *Then* Abe. And that would be a considerable feat.

They made a very bad pair to handle. Abe quick—Louis watching. Between them, a damn good reason to get the hell out of Bristolton.

Pronto.

It was possible, after all, that Mister Manstein, the livery man, might have a prime plug dirt cheap. And if he didn't, no harm in looking. No harm in looking for a cold beer and a ham sandwich, instead, maybe having a jaw with the boys in some saloon.

A sensible man didn't mind running, if he had to.

Scurrying, was something else.

# CHAPTER THIRTEEN

Manstein was a thick-shouldered man with colorless eyes and white hair he kept cut short. A kid had shown Lacy the way back to the livery corral; Manstein's son, probably.

When he got back there, Lacy saw that the Dutchman ran a freight outfit as well. Three big wide-wheel wagons were parked past the corral, and a bunch of broad-rumped draft horses were haltered off down a line like cavalry mounts. It gave Lacy two notions. First, that Manstein had likely been a cavalryman (a double-chevron sergeant, probably), and second, that as a freighter, a man with a substantial business, Manstein was certain to be a prime pain in the ass on a horse deal.

Right, both counts.

"The old Seventh, when it *was* the Seventh. . ." Manstein gave Lacy a look, like maybe he was the one had sent the regiment downhill. "You were a trooper?"

"I scouted a little," Lacy said.

He got a snort out of the liveryman for that. The snort said that half the trash in Texas claimed to have scouted for the Army one time or another.

"For Gilchrist, one campaign. And for Lewis in Oklahoma."

"Do say?" Manstein said. He had hardly any Dutch accent left at all. "Oklahoma, huh? You go back damn near as far as I do!" No more snorting, now. "I heard Lewis was blind as a bat. That so?"

"He wore spectacles, but he seemed to see the Indians fair enough."

Manstein grunted. "Blind as a bat, I heard," he said.

Fairly started off with a lie, since he had never seen Colonel Gilchrist or Major Turley Lewis in his life, Lacy set himself for the storm of lies that Manstein was about to send his way concerning the crow-bait shaking around his corral.

Lacy'd been eying the saddle stock since the kid had shown him the yard, and Manstein had been watching him watching all during the conversation about the old Seventh.

"You looking for a horse?"

"Looking at 'em is more like it. No hurry to buy." And right there is where Lacy had old Manstein across a barrel. Because he didn't *want* any of the freighter's horses. The one he wanted was a tall gray thoroughbred, with a mouthy, drunk lawyer up on him.

"Well, here's a prime one. A prime one!" He'd steered Lacy over to the corral rail, and was pointing to a slab-sided black with a wall eye. "Nothing to look at at all, mind you. Take a *horseman* to see that animal's staying power. Strength and speed—that's what those lines say to a man that knows his business!"

Lacy glanced to see if Manstein was keeping a straight face, and he was. Solemn as a judge. A good business man, sure enough.

Lacy pointed across the corral to a heavy-barreled sorrel, but before he could open his mouth—"Not for sale!" Manstein said. And his mouth clamped down hard. Not for sale, and that was that. He'd known all the time that Lacy was too smart, too knowing to be fooled by the flat-sided black. Well, Lacy might have picked out the diamond gem of his stock. The toughest, fastest, best-bred pony Bristolton had seen in months. Lacy had proved sharp, all right, but that horse was not for sale. Period. That sorrel horse was too *good* to sell.

Period.

"How much?" Lacy said.

Not for sale,

"How much?"

No use even talking about it. That pony has been bred from a champion racer and a Sioux war stallion. No use even talking price. That horse was meant for a gift for the President, if he came to Texas. The Governor, if the President didn't show.

"How much?"

Why talk about it? An ordinary man couldn't even afford a horse like that. Why bother to even talk about it?

"How much?"

Well, never really thought about putting a cash price on Ace. People in Bristolton called that horse "Ace." People were talking about racing him in the Cup race at Austin.

"How much?"

Well, seeing that Lacy was damn near an ex-trooper. Seeing that he was an old campaigner. Hell, he and Manstein both knew what an Indian arrow sounded like hissing past your ear. Seeing that. That they'd served together, damn near.

"How much?"

"Five-hundred dollars, gold."

Lacy kept his face straight, but it took some doing. "My," he said, "that sure *must* be some horse. A good deal too rich for my blood, I can tell you that!"

"Well now," Manstein said, "of course that horse still needs its training rounded-off. It's perfect saddle-broke, of course, but there is some fine training still to be done." He gave it some thought.

"Too rich for my blood."

"Now just a minute," Manstein said. "I said there was still a little training to be done with that animal." He gave it more thought. "I think. . . I *think*. . . I might let it go to an expert in horse-flesh. . . a man I could depend on to polish that fine animal up to its perfection."

"How much?"

"Three-hundred and fifty dollars, gold."

Lacy shook his head. "Oh, lordy," he said. "And I've always sort of dreamed of owning a horse of that caliber, too. A horse with all those fine points, I mean, not like those straight-shouldered nags you see so much of these days."

"By God, sir," Manstein said, "it does a man's heart good to meet a man that *knows* a horse when he sees him. Hell." He shook his head. "Mark me down for a damn fool if you wish. I'll sell you that top-crust horse for two-hundred and fifty dollars flat! And I'll take paper money, too!"

"Great God in Zion," Lacy said, looking sadder than ever. "To come so close! So close to being able to purchase that handsome horse. And just not quite be able to swing it."

Manstein gave him a sharp look, but Lacy took care to keep looking longingly across the corral at the heavy-barreled sorrel.

"That horse is worth two-hundred and fifty dollars," Manstein said, a little sharp.

"No doubt about that," Lacy said. "Worth more than that, I'd say." He sighed.

Manstein gave it some thought.

"Of course, a fine saddle and bridle goes with the animal, all well broken-in."

"I've got a saddle," Lacy said.

"Two-hundred dollars," Manstein said, and he gave Lacy a sergeant's look.

"Damn it!" Lacy said. "And me just short!"

Manstein gritted his teeth. "Well, I'm not selling that horse for less than two-hundred," he said. There was more German accent in his talking now.

"Don't blame you," Lacy said, and he turned to go. "Say, you don't mind if I come by sometimes? Just to look at him?"

Manstein glared at him, his face flushed red under the crop of white hair. "Mister," he said, "you can do whatever you damn please." And he stomped away to his office at the back of the livery, went in, and slammed the door shut behind him.

Lacy thought it a fair day's work. Come it might happen that he'd have to buy the sorrel. A slug if he'd ever seen one. He should be able to get the bill of sale for one-fifty, tops.


Lacy walked back down Main Street, into the dusty slanting light of the afternoon sun. The street was even more crowded than it had been. Spring round ups were bringing every ranch cook and wagoner in for flour and side pork, posts and wire. Bringing the buyers in, too, to look over the calf crops, do their first bids and veal buying, talk to the foremen and drovers about the stock, judging their bids for the finished herds.

The hands, and the buyers, and the hangers-on, the store clerks and merchants, the markers and acreage men, the wire salesmen and whiskey drummers, low-lifes, bet-sellers come up from South Street, farmers, plowboys, and all their kin, kids and grannies and bonneted wives.

A heap of folks.

And a big deputy strolling along like a Philadelphia copper, with a badge like a wagon wheel, a Russian-model Smith & Wesson .44, and the tail of a slung-shot hanging out of his back pocket. Lacy gave him a careful look as he walked by. A big man, with a pair of shoulders—and a belly—like a mule. A crusher. No gunman.

A fellow to keep young drovers in line when they'd had a snoot-full on Saturday night. For more serious business, Lacy supposed—the vigilante committee that Jeff Compton had spoken about. A couple dozen men in their forties, men who'd seen the elephant, coming with carbines and shot-guns. For more serious business.

And what they couldn't handle. . .well, the Rangers would come riding up. and they'd handle it just fine.

A town old in the ways of trouble. Gun-trouble, anyway. They'd find the railroad harder to handle. Find the Central Cattle Company harder to handle, too. It had probably already dug a money-tooth into the town. Into the judge and magistrate, into the marshal, for sure.

Angle Iron, all those old spreads still run—those of them the big winter hadn't broken—more like Mex *haciendas* than American businesses. They were all dead meat to the bankers, and high-price silver, and Morgan and his friends in Chicago and New York City.

The old ways were going fast.


He turned in under a fresh-painted Dry Goods & Sundries sign, opened a door paned with squares of glass, which rang a small bell over his head, and walked into the shadows of the store.

Four men were sitting at a cold potbelly stove, looking as though they were willing to wait for winter there, till the stove was lit again. They were dipping snuff out of an old tomato can. Two of them were old, but the other two were young men. One of these, with his black hair parted in the middle and slicked down flat, stood up and gave Lacy a nod. He had a storekeeper's apron on.

"What do you need, Mister?"

"A base-ball bat, if you have one," Lacy said. "Hickory for choice, but ash will do."

"Damn! Is a game gettin' up?" one of the old men said. He took a dip, tucked some fresh in under his lip, and snorted the rest.

"Not this afternoon," Lacy said. "Maybe this week-end."

"I don't carry ash at all," the store-keeper said, going behind his counter. "It's got no whip to it." He walked down the counter into the darkness at the back of the store, rattled around in a corner, and came walking back, the bib of his apron white in the shadows. "Now, this is the prime article, right here," he said. "Look at this and tell me that's not so."

Lacy took the bat and hefted it. It was a fine piece of hardwood, with thin grain laced down it in long, narrow "V's." Lacy stepped back to get clear, gripped the bat, and swung it hard, feeling the weight of it haul at his shoulder.

"Prime article," said the shop-keeper.

"Let me see that bat," the old man with the snuff just tucked in said.

Lacy went over and handed it to him, and the old man lifted the wood to smell at it. "Weather-seasoned," he said. "None of this fire-dried stuff people will palm off on you." He weighed the bat in his hands. "Homer," he said.

122

"Who's making these bats for you?"

"Doctor Seligman," the store-keeper said, "you know damn well that's a Missouri bat straight out of St. Louis."

"There's a man in McAllen cuts 'em just as fine," the old man said.

"Say what?" the other old man said. "A base-ball bat that fine out of McAllen? You been smoking that Chinese tar again, Doc?"

"Must have been," the young man sitting at the stove said. "What would he have been cuttin' it out of? Cotton-wood?"

The old man, Seligman, handed the bat back to Lacy. "Please, Norris, do try not to reveal your ignorance to a stranger in town. It reflects upon the entire community." He bent over to spit some juice into a mason jar beside his chair. "It so happens that Kerr County grows some of the finest mountain hardwood in the South. And a choice selection of that timber goes straight to McAllen and into the workshop of Henry Busbee, who can carve a cabinet or turn a bat with any man in the nation. Bar none."

"You're shittin' us, ain't you, Doc?" the other old man said. He winked at Lacy. "Doc here is a damned outrageous liar, Mister. You'll learn that's true, if you stick around town."

"Could be," Lacy said. "But he's talking straight enough about Henry Busbee. I heard of him in Montana. Say he can make a dresser agreeable as a Kansas City tart."

"How's that?"

"You put two dollars on a Busbee dresser, it'll pop its drawers for you."

It wasn't much, but they enjoyed it.

"I do like a man with a dirty mouth," Doctor Seligman said, and reached up to shake hands. They introduced themselves all round. Doctor Seligman. *Human*, not horse doctor, he said. Morris Patch was the other old man, the town notary, retired. The young man was the storekeeper's brother, Norris.

"Passing through, Mister Lacy?" he said.

Lacy nodded. "Just passing through." He thought about it and thought, why not?

"I've got a short-time job at Miss Maynard's," he said. "While Big William is sick."

They all looked at him for a moment.

"I suppose his malaria came back on him," Seligman said.

"That's it."

"Well," Seligman said with a sigh, "I'll have to look in on him tonight. Malaria's tricky."

"Ho, ho," old Patch said. "Pardon my laughin'. We know what you're goin' down there for, Doc. And it sure ain't to tend that big nigger!" He dipped himself some snuff.

"Morris is past it," Seligman said, smiling up at Lacy. "It makes him a mite bitter to see others going to their pleasure."

"So you say," Patch said, but he looked some put out.

"The guard there, huh?" Norris said, looking at Lacy.

"Not too much of that, I hope," Lacy said. "I intend to be playing some poker."

"Do tell?" the shopkeeper said, still standing behind his counter. "And would you be a professional?"

"I was," Lacy said. "Pretty rusty now, I'm afraid."

Seligman looked up. "You speak like a gentleman, Mister Lacy."

"I was," Lacy said. "Pretty rusty now, I'm afraid."

It wasn't much, but they enjoyed it.

Lacy paid for the bat—one dollar even—said his good-days, and left.

As he went out the door, he heard Norris ask old Seligman if there really was a great base-ball bat maker in McAllen.

"How the hell would I know, Norris?" the doctor said.

# CHAPTER FOURTEEN

Lacy had lost $52.

Fair enough for the first night; and he might make up some of it before the night was over. Partly it was policy—giving the suckers a break to start—and partly it was bad playing. He and old Doc Seligman and a couple of cattle buyers from Kansas had been playing five-card for a while, then switched to high-card draw. It was the draw that had cost Lacy his $52. He still had his card-sense; it was his people-sense that had rusted. He figured Seligman fast enough: he was a smart old son-of-a-bitch who liked to take chances. But the cattle buyers were solid card players, and he'd missed their bluffs and buys more than once. He had to play careful poker, too; he couldn't plunge on down a streak, not with less than $90 to lose.

It made a man uneasy, playing with short money.

They were playing at Miss Maynard's back parlor table, with the big fringed shawl that had covered it neatly folded up and put away by Sarah.

Miss Maynard had introduced Lacy to some of the regulars, substantial citizens, every one, and had done a good job of it, letting them know that Lacy was (or had been) a professional, and calling the game just a try-out, to see if her valued clients cared for it. The men seemed to like the idea well enough, at least they didn't grumble at it. And if Lacy kept losing, they'd like it even better.

Lacy had been right about some men preferring to look at the life than live it. The men he was playing with hadn't gone up to the girls. Nathan Simes was the name of the older cattle buyer, a red-faced man in a fine Chicago suit. The other man was a slender sissy named Maxwell. Maxwell had finicky ways—he'd sent a beef sandwich back to the kitchen because it had gristle in it—but he was a dangerous poker player. One of the rare amateurs who played like a professional. He played for money, and not for anything else. Not to be the winner, not to have something to crow about, not to beat other men down.

Just for the money.

He was the one giving Lacy the most trouble.

There were ways to handle a player like that. Take a wild bet now and then, to unsettle him. Bid up a bluff once or twice to keep him uneasy about your game. And play him dead straight all the other hands.

There were ways, if you had the cash to back your play.

Right now, Maxwell was holding the game's high hand surer than hell, and sitting across from Lacy as calm as pudding. That shade *too* calm. Maxwell had curly blond hair, with macassar oil on it, and a fine gold watch-chain, studded with tiny pearls, across his vest.

He was a dandy and he was waiting to see if Lacy was fool enough to stick to the pot the way old Seligman had just done. It was a prime occasion to play the fool, and lose some money to him, but Lacy couldn't spare the cash.

"I'm out."

Maxwell didn't seem to mind. He was a polite fellow.

They all were. Responsible men, family men, most of them. None of your roaring boys here; that was for the cribs further down South Street.

Lacy heard the knocker on the front door. He hadn't had much in the guarding line to do, so far. Stood by Miss Maynard once, while she warned off a drunk drummer with a fat white tomcat sitting on his shoulder. Poker and rare beef sandwiches, most of the evening. A man could certainly get used to the work.

Whoever was knocking, was knocking hard. Lacy heard Sarah's voice out in the hall. Then Miss Maynard's. Miss Maynard sounded upset.

"Excuse me, boys. Deal me out of the next hand."

He pushed his chair, got up, and walked through the parlor door out into the hall. Sarah and Miss Maynard were standing at the half-open door. Trying to close it.

Somebody outside had their boot in the door frame.

"Get off my porch! Drovers are not welcome in this house!" Miss Maynard's voice was a furious squeak.

"Git on out of the way, yuh damn ol' trout!" Laughter from the porch. "It ain't yore ol' gash we're after!" More laughter.

Lacy walked to the door, bent to pick up the base-ball bat from the umbrella stand, moved Miss Maynard and Sarah aside with his left hand, then raised the bat over his head with both hands, and brought it down as hard as he could onto the toe of the intruding boot.

When the man outside screamed in agony, Lacy kicked the door wide open and went out onto the porch with the bat up and back and swinging.

Things seemed to slow down for him, as they always did when he was in a fight. Less, usually, for this kind of a scramble, than when it was guns.

As he came through the door, he saw one drover hopping

to the side holding his foot in his hand. Another cowpoker, a squat young man with bandy legs and a freckled face, was standing his ground. There were two others behind him.

Freckle-face looked a little tough, glaring under the porch-lamp, his hand going for the pistol stuck in his belt.

Lacy brought the bat down hard, full swing at the cowboy's collarbone. There was an instant, as the bat came down, when the drover might have made his draw—if he was fast enough. But it took a stern man to stand still under the swing of a base-ball bat, and make his draw, and take his shot.

Freckle-face tried to dodge away his hand coming up off his gun to try and ward the blow.

Too slow.

Lacy hit him very hard, and felt bone break under the bat.

Freckle-face went to his knees, and Lacy kneed him in the face, and went on after the others. He caught the third one turning, hit him high across the back, and knocked him over the porch rail into Miss Maynard's flower bed.

While that one was groaning in the flowers, the fourth ranny—young and skinny, with a nose like a buzzard's beak—ran down the walk a little way, then turned and pulled out a butcher knife.

Lacy went down the steps and at him at a run, the St. Louis bat making whuffling noises as he swung it.

The boy stood for a moment, his thin face shiny with sweat in the moonlight. Lacy reached out for him with the bat, and he broke and turned and ran, still holding onto the butcher knife. Its blade glittered as he ran away, stumbling through the fence gate and taking off down South Street as if Lacy were just behind him and catching up.

Lacy stood on the walk and watched him go, then he turned and started back up to the porch, the bat cocked back and ready. The hopping drover vauled over the porch rail as if there was nothing wrong with his foot at all, and he and the boy from the flower bed tore off around the side of the house and out into the night, in the general direction of Fort Worth.

Freckle-face was sitting up on the porch floor crying and holding his shoulder. He looked younger crying than he had reaching for his pistol.

Old Doctor Seligman was standing in the doorway. "Goodness gracious," he said, "you *are* a sudden man, Mister Lacy."


By the time Sarah and Seligman had taken the crying cowpoke out to the kitchen so Doc could rig a sling for him, and Lacy had accepted the congratulations of all the comfortable sports presently in the parlor, and the girls had giggled the news throughout the house, the two cattle buyers had decided they'd had enough poker anyway, and Maxwell was settling into a game of cribbage with a rancher named Ordrey. No chance at getting any money back from him. Maxwell was a smart sissy, and no mistake. The other buyer, Simes, appeared to be taking heavily to drink; probably trying to get his nerve up for one of the girls.

Silky came drifting through—she'd just short-timed a harness salesman named McMurty—and gave Lacy a wink and Simes a come-hither look. It only seemed to scare him deeper into his whiskey and siphon-soda, so she shrugged and drifted the other way, where two town storekeepers were sitting talking freight charges.

It occured to Lacy that Simes and Maxwell might be sweet on each other, going to houses more for appearances than any fun they got out of it. He'd seen a lot of that.

Whatever, it looked as though the poker line had about

run out for the night. Probably that piece of bat-work had scared some of the clients off the game. Probably figured him for something fierce, smacking those drunk cow-boys the way he had.

Lacy'd just resigned himself to a losing night, and was beginning to think the whole notion not so satisfactory, when the front door knocker started started rapping again.

This time, though, it wasn't trouble.

It was a potbellied surveyor with Burnside whiskers, and a big red-faced man with considerable liquor on his breath.

The lawyer, Talbot.

The man who owned the gray.


Talbot was drunk, but not drunk enough. He remembered Lacy from that meeting out on the prairie, and didn't appear to like what he remembered.

It would be too good to be true, to get the man into a poker game and wind up with that gray horse. And, as the night went on, it seemed to Lacy to be damned well too good to be true.

He had his game with Talbot, all right. The town surveyor with the whiskers was anxious to play, fancied himself a card-man, and Talbot went along with it, but only after he'd gone upstairs with a short, heavy girl named Patience.

Lacy had his game with them, when Talbot came back downstairs—and they cleaned him out.

It wasn't that they were so damn good, although Talbot was a strong, careful player, even with all the bourbon he was taking on board. They just ran Lacy out of money; and it was a damn short run. One bid-up on a pat hand did it. Lacy had four of a kind, and he tried like hell to stick with the bets as they went up. But it was a no-raise-limit game, and Talbot, the surveyor, and the other players—a horse rancher named Bierce—raised him over and out. Lacy gave up his seat to one of the shopkeepers, and walked out into the hall and down to the kitchen and outside.

It was a cool, clear night. The smell of sagebrush and woodsmoke. The moon was down already, but the starlight was bright enough to see by.

Lacy went to the outhouse and had a good piss. First day—or night, anyway—at work, and already dead broke. His good idea about the poker had turned out to be not such a good idea. Miss Maynard wouldn't be pleased. Her cut—for tonight's play—would be a fat nothing.

He walked back inside the house to find her.


The old lady was upstairs, muttering in the big walk-in linen closet. Lacy could sympathize. Linen was the heavy cost in running a house. Linen, and money to pay off the law.

Miss Maynard was standing on a stepladder, cursing softly and counting through a stack of sheets. She rolled a cold eye at him.

"You're making no money for me, Mister Lacy." Then she went back to her counting.

A customer was coming down the hall, laughing with one of the girls. Lacy stepped into the closet and closed the door behind him. The only light was a candle set behind a safety glass in a saucer.

"I want to borrow some money from you, Miss Maynard."

She snorted. "I'll wager that you do," she said.

"A hundred dollars would do me," Lacy said.

"I'll wager it would," she said.

"You'd be paid back tomorrow."

132

She finished her count of the sheets, and climbed down the ladder to face him. She looked like a little banty hen. "How in the world will you pay me back, Mister Lacy, and why in the world should I lend you a penny?"

"You'd be paid. How, is my business."

"And why should I risk it at all, Mister Lacy?"

"Because I would be personally beholden to you, if you did."

The old lady looked up at him, squinting sharply in the candlelight. "And what the hell would that mean for me, Mister?" she said.

"Maybe a great deal, one day, if bad trouble should come to you."

"Strikes me that you *are* bad trouble, Mister Lacy," she said. Then she winked, and as she did, Lacy saw, for a fraction of a second, the tiny, pretty, clever little whore she must have been as a girl. She poked him in the belly with a bony little forefinger. "One-hundred dollars tonight. And by noon tomorrow, I'll expect you to put one-hundred-and-twenty-five dollars back into my hand." She brushed past him, opened the door, and went out into the hall. "Well," she said. "Come on and get your money. *My* money, I should say!"

As he followed her down the corridor, Lacy realized that the tough little madam liked him. She'd probably enjoyed seeing those cow-boys scramble away from the base-ball bat.

He got back downstairs with the hundred dollars, worried that Talbot might have cleared out of the place while he was upstairs.

Talbot was there, only a little drunker. He and the old surveyor were singing along with the player piano. A couple of the other men were singing along with them. *Jeannie*

*With The Light Brown Hair.*

They made a fair quartet, singing together.

When the singing was over, Talbot and his friend were willing enough to sit down and play again. Why not? Lacy'd given them a contribution already. Bierce had left, but a wire freighter named McCauley was willing to sit in.

"Looking for revenge, Mister Lacy?" Talbot said. The lawyer looked cheerful and relaxed, doing nicely at a certain level of liquor.

"No, Mister Talbot," Lacy said. "I'm after your horse."

"Are you, by God?" Talbot said. He laughed. "Then you have your work cut out. Rain is a thousand dollar horse."

"Rain?" And that was his color, right enough.

"That's his name," Talbot said," raised by Colonel Martin Chavez of Lexington, Kentucky. Bred by the Caisson out of Frisky Queen."

"Stop braggin' yore horse, Mister Talbot," McCauley said, "and le's play some cards."

Silky came into the parlor, looking tired. It was getting late; the house was quieting down, smelling of cigar smoke and perfume and sweat.

"Your deal, Mister Lacy," Talbot said. "You have a long way to go to get to my horse."

# CHAPTER FIFTEEN

Lacy woke at noon.

Not in the fancy room he'd first had Silky in. Miss Maynard had moved his things out of that room, pronto. She'd given him a cot in a narrow storage room beside the back porch. Big William and Sarah slept in a crib just like it across the way.

It wasn't fancy. There were crates of everything from turnips to laundry soap stacked beside the cot. The cot was narrow, too. There sure as hell wasn't room on it for Lacy *and* a sturdy tired-out whore. Silky lay crowded half over him, snoring like a pug dog and smelling of sweet soap.

Lacy thought about last night's poker. He hadn't won the gray horse. Not quite.

But he'd sure as hell given Talbot and his surveying friend a whipping. Over six-hundred dollars from Talbot. Almost three-hundred from his friend. The wire freighter, McCauley, had gotten a good piece of that, too.

Lacy had figured what he'd need—and sliced off Miss Maynard's cut, and what he owed her—and had offered Talbot six hundred dollars for the gray.

Talbot had given him a polite "No." The man was a cool enough loser.

Well, there was still time enough to turn horse-thief.

Silky murmured in her sleep, and commenced to droll a little on his shoulder. She was a sweet girl. And a hard worker. Miss Maynard had a pearl in this one.

And it turned out she hadn't done so badly with Lacy, either. He wouldn't be lucky enough to—hit all the customers as hard as he had Talbot last night. Even so, the old lady would make money on the deal for sure in the next few days. And he'd have a chance to buy that gray. Silky'd said that Talbot was up to his ears buying railroad stock, like half the fools and plungers west of the Mississippi. Could be, that a few hundred more might persuade him to sell, and still leave Lacy enough to ride down into Mexico like a gent. The old Don would be happy enough to see him. It had been years since he'd helped the old bandit steal about a quarter of Sonora.

Years.

Years enough to find and lose a ranch on Rifle River. And a girl—found. . . and then lost, too. Mister Famous Gunfighter. Well, he'd damned near fought himself out of places to go: hanged and shot his way out of that mountain ranch, sure enough. And did the same in Idaho. Cost himself a whole new life, in Idaho. And the woman to go with it. Doing what had to be done? Maybe. And maybe grabbing a chance to show off his famous gunplay, grabbing a chance to prove what a special fellow he was—with a pistol in his hand.

A leopard can change his name: changing his spots is a harder go.

A hell of a harder go.

Lacy gently eased out from under the sleeping girl, got his feet on the floor and stood up, stark naked, in the bright bars of sunlight shining through the crib's slats.

He dressed quietly, and walked out onto the porch in his stocking feet, holding his boots in his hand so he wouldn't wake Silky up.

It was a perfect day, sunny as gold, the sky as blue as English china. He looked out past the clothes-lines and washtubs. There were two other houses a pistol shot away, one out to the left, a little white clapboard house with a garden over there. The lady of the house must have insisted on some flowers to accompany the melons and tomatoes and snap-beans.

The other house, more a shack than a house, was straight out back and farther away. Unpainted, gray as slate.

There was nothing else behind Miss Maynard's, except the waist-high bud-green fog of spring mesquite, creosote, and paint brush. That mild green rolled right out to the horizon, bar a dip away to the old riverbed alongside the first buildings of the town.

Lacy heard prairie hens chuckling in the brush. Sitting their first clutch of eggs, and mighty proud of it. He heard songbirds far off, down in the river gully. Some still-damp place had drawn them down to it. Probably, a man could dig down through the sand for a yard and find some winter wet lingering there. Be gone by summer.

He walked back across the porch, and pushed open the kitchen door. Miss Maynard kept an Irish woman to cook for her people, which was different from the way most people did it. You'd usually find an Indian woman or a colored woman cooking in a house.

Mrs. Collins was a short, thick-shouldered woman with hands like a man's. She was a good cook, Silky had said, but a drinker with a temper to watch out for by nightfall. Lacy walked into the kitchen and took a chair at the end of the table. Only one of the girls was still eating breakfast. A

137

Mexican girl. Lacy had seen her the night before, taking the men upstairs in double-quick time. She was a nice-looking girl, like most of Miss Maynard's.

"*Buenas dias.*"

She gave him a pleasant smile and a nod. Nothing to say, though.

"What'll you be havin' for your breakfast, Mister Lacy?" Mrs. Collins stood by her stove, looking at Lacy in a friendly enough fashion.

"Four eggs, ham if you have it—"

"It'll have to be pork-belly bacon, Mister Lacy."

"Okay. And potatoes, pan-fried."

"Comin' right at ya," said Mrs. Collins, and she lifted a stove-lid, poked up her fire, and set to work.


Mrs. Collins was a fine cook. Lacy finished the plateful, and wiped it clean with his fifth biscuit. Mrs. Collins, who appeared to appreciate a good appetite, came over then and served him out another egg, another long slice of bacon, and another spoonful of potatoes. Then she stood back to see if he could handle it.

Silky came yawning into the kitchen while he was still working on the potatoes. She had a fancy red dressing gown on, with green Chinese dragons embroidered on it.

"Just coffee and syrup and biscuits for me, Mrs. Collins," she said, and she sat down beside Lacy at the table, and reached down behind him, out of sight of Mrs. Collins and the Mexican girl, and pinched him on the ass.

It occurred to Lacy that maybe he'd given Silky too much rope. She was acting like a damned barrelhouse bride.


After breakfast, as scrubbed, fed, and fucked as any gay-life mack, Lacy strolled down South Street to Jeff Compton's shop.

Another bright Texas day, coming on to frying-hot. Nobody much strolling South Street. Too early for the crib-girls to be taking the air. Too early for the gamblers and markers, as well. Kids still in school. Drummers up on Main, doing their rounds.

Some dogs out, though, lying in the ruts with their tongues hanging, eyes squinted half-shut in the sunshine. One by one, down the dusty road, the dogs got up and out of the way to let a buckboard by, then strolled back to their flops, stretched in the dirt, and let their tongues hang out again.

Lacy's bootsteps reverberated on the boardwalk; nobody else's weight on the planks to keep them from booming. He could smell dust and sagebrush, but there wasn't a breath of breeze blowing in from the prairie.

He stepped down into the street, and crossed over to Compton's shop.

The door was open; the bell jingled as he went in. Nobody was in front, but Lacy heard someone moving around in back of the store, so he let the bell bring Jeff in while he took a gander at the leather goods. He saw the saddlebags, folded on a shelf at the back of the counter, and noticed a handsome wallet, that was new, or he'd missed it first visit. It might do, if he had a few more days winning at Miss Maynard's. It was a fine piece of work—looked like pigskin—with small lacing around the edges.

''Mister Lacy!'' Jeff came wheeling his bath chair in from the back. Last time, Lacy hadn't noticed how old Compton had gotten; hadn't seen all the gray in his hair. It hadn't been so many years, but a cripple has to age faster than a whole man. More weighing him down, more pain, more trouble. Lacy supposed that losing Virginia had put most of those years on Jeff Compton.

"Morning, Jeff. Come for those saddle-bags."

"Damn, Lacy, you must have made your money mighty fast."

"Dealing some poker at Miss Maynard's," Lacy said, counting out the cash for the saddlebags. Compton laid them on the counter; they looked as fine as Lacy'd thought they had. Would look prime on that gray—if Talbot would come back to play some more cards.

"Do me a favor, Jeff?"

"You name it." Jeff was cheerier today, not having come close to getting his head blown off

"You got a boy can deliver these to Miss Maynard's for me?"

"I do. A little greaser named Manuel. A real nice boy. He brings me my dinner—his Ma's a hell of a cook—and he'll take 'em right over for you."

"Okay. And why don't you measure me up for that buckskin vest, while I'm here."

"Hell, yes," Compton said, dug under his counter for a tape measure, and came squeaking around from behind the counter to go to work. "You want the same pattern as this old one?"

"Just the same."

"Fringes that long?"

"Sure. They don't get in my way, and hide string can come in handy."

"Shit," Compton said, reaching up to hold the tape to the point of Lacy's shoulders, "you just like fancy fixin's. No reason to be ashamed of that."

Lacy sighed. Let a man put a tape measure on you, and he was one-up every time. "You got bone buttons for the vest?"

"Damn right," Compton said. "You're goin' to look fine as a double eagle before I'm through!"

The saddlebags bought, measured for the vest up and down and sideways, Lacy strolled north up to Main Street, considering a cold beer. It might do, as well, to pick up a box of cartridges for the Sharps. Hulls for the big buffalo gun were getting hard to find—all hand-loaded by some local fellow for those who still used the big pieces—And then, perhaps a drop in for a haircut and shave. Follow that with another visit to Manstein's. Keep hooking that square-head hard enough, he might give a horse away just to get Lacy off his back. Just in case Talbot didn't come through with the gray.

Main Street was busier than South had been. Business people didn't mind the heat of the day as much as the over-the-line folks did. Early to bed, early to rise. A big freight train moving out of Manstein's down the block. Four long wagons piled high, loads canvased and tied down hard. Be a load off Manstein's mind, getting that lot rolling and off. A good time to go and play purchase with him. A must-be-done after the hair cut.

"Say there, now, it's the redoubtable Lacy! The Hector of South Street!" Old Doc Seligman came shoving past a pair of drummers, a bulge of snuff under his lower lip. He was spry, for a man that old, swinging a little brown doctor's bag in his hand.

"A pretty piece of work with those drovers, Sir. A pretty piece of work!" He squinted up into Lacy's face. "Now, you know, I hadn't seen that scar of yours by sunlight. There's nothing like full daylight for a proper view of any condition." Without any "by your leave," the old man reached up and commenced to poke at the scar across Lacy's left cheek. A couple of people, passing by on the boardwalk, stopped to see what Seligman was up to. It was always of interest to watch a medical man at work. Lacy didn't know how to set the doctor down without hurting his feelings. He needn't have worried about it.

"I suppose," the old man said, poking and pulling at the scar, "I suppose you'd like me to set off straight for hell, instead of making you a spectacle for these—" He turned and gave the loafers a hard glance. "—these congenital idiots. However," and he was back to poking, "one doesn't often see such a near separation of the trigeminal with such limited effect." He let go of Lacy's face. "You have a little droop there. Some lack of feeling on that side of your mouth?"

"Some."

"Well, you're damn lucky, boy," Seligman said. "I've known men cut there to have the food drop out of their mouths every time they tried to eat. And be in some considerably terrible pain and discomfort from it, too. That nerve is nothing to fool with."

"No sir," Lacy said, feeling like a fool for these people to look at. There was getting to be a fair crowd around them now.

"Well, I can't stand around here all day, Lacy!" the old man said, as if Lacy had begged him for his attention. And Seligman hefted his little brown bag, said, "Again, well done with that base-ball bat!" And went stumping off down the walk, pushing people out of the way.

Lacy went on his way, hearing some chuckles from the loafers behind him—Seligman seemed known for conducting these public examinations every now and then.

"Lucky he didn't charge ya!" one of the men called after him as he went. Lacy found himself feeling with his tongue for the slightly raised ridge of the scar inside his cheek. The slug had damned near torn that side of his face off.

Shannon. Small, quiet, blond man going gray. He'd worn buckskin, too. Shannon. One of the good ones. One of the best. He'd killed Slim Wilson out of Cheyenne.

And damned near killed Lacy, too. Or *Lea*, as he was calling himself then. Damned near.

To hell with all that. To hell with past times! A hair-cut and a shave, that's what he was heading for, now.

He went down some steps, across an alley—a couple of pigs were rooting at a trash pile in there—and up the steps on the other side to the next boardwalk.

There was some commotion up ahead.

Couple of men were having some kind of tussle in the street.

Cowboys. Kicking up a lot of dust.

Lacy stepped in between a store clerk and a piss-smelling drunk to get a better look.

It was the Australian, Harry Pierce.

He had hold of Buddy Manugian, saying something hard to him. "Stay out." Something like that.

When the boy moved to get past him, the Australian hit him in the face and knocked him down.

# CHAPTER SIXTEEN

Lacy was surprised enough for a moment, not to jump right down in the street and get into it. He hadn't thought of Pierce as a bully.

Once the boy was down, though, the Australian didn't try to put the boot to him. Instead, he turned away, climbed up onto the boardwalk, pushed his way through the crowd, and walked through the bat-wing doors of a saloon called the Two-bits.

Lacy stepped into the street, but Buddy was already back on his feet, his face white as paper and blood running out of his nose.

"You all right, boy?"

Buddy Manugian didn't answer him. Instead, the boy turned to a tied-off horse—it was his done-in pony, Blackie—reached over the saddle-bow, and dragged the old Henry up out of the boot.

Lacy stepped in and took him by the arm. "You won't need that to fight a friend, will you, Bud?" The boy tried to twist free, but Lacy held him.

"Listen," the boy said, his face screwed up like a baby

about to cry, "you get out of my way! Abe Bothwell's got Pete in there and he's callin' him names. He's goin' to kill him, Mister Lacy!"

Pierce had knocked the boy down to keep him out of Bothwell's fight.

"In the Two-bits?"

"Please let me go, Mister Lacy!" He tried to wrestle away.

"Shut your mouth and stand still a minute!" The loafers looking on were getting a rare show with all this whoop-de-doo. It was all the worse kind of luck. Somebody must have taken the leash off the Bothwells.

And no put-in of his, either. It would be Pete Stern and the Australian against the gunmen in there. No chance at all, of course. . . Surprising not to have heard the shooting already. Bothwell must be playing with them.

"God damn you!" the boy said, and he stamped down hard on Lacy's foot. It hurt like the devil, and the boy took his chance, kicked free, jumped up onto the board-walk, and was gone into the Two-bits.

The fat was in the fire and cooking hot.

Lacy turned and ran down the street to the alley entrance, and on up the alley, kicking a pig out of the way and running hard. Now what in God's good name am I doing? Do I have a choice? Give me a minute to think of some damn choice! Stern and Pierce can take their chances. Men grown, and with guns on. Stern likes a fight: let him have one, then. The Australian's seen the elephant—his choice, too.

Lacy got to the end of the alley, jumped up on the board-walk there, pushed two women out of the way, and stooped to drag his boots off, got the left off and was tugging at the right, hopping toward the back door of the Two-bit.

A dandy smooth dodger, was Buckskin Frank. He got the right boot off, saving the Arkansas toothpick by sliding the blade into the back of his gunbelt. Oh, yes, you're a dandy. Doc should see this.

The women were clucking like angry hens behind him, and he reached the back door of the Two-bits in his stocking feet. Likely some drunk would make off with those boots.

The door was open, but there was a cloth-screen door on the hinges behind it. The muslin was stained and sagging. Oh, what are you doing, you damn fool? The kid is nothing to you at all.

He pushed the door open gently with his left hand, and stepped into the dark.

Voices. A voice. And light at the end of the hall.

Lacy reached down to make sure the keeper-loop was off the Colt's. Getting old. . . getting slow. . . surprised at how fast the luck had run out. Just another few days, a little more money. . . He'd have ridden out just right.

*That God-damned kid.*

He went on down the hall, keeping to the edge so the boards wouldn't creak too much. Likely get a splinter in his foot, die of blood poisoning.

The voice was clearer. Abe Bothwell. Joking. Showing off.

Louis would be there, too. Watching.

He'd have to kill Louis first.


Louis was watching. Lacy saw him from the doorway into the barroom. Louis was watching. But not his own back.

The bulky man was sitting at a small table just a few feet from the hall doorway watching Abe talking by the bar. Lacy saw the three drovers standing in a row in front of a table across the room. Pete Stern was standing a little out front. His gut stuck out, his fat hand held just clear of the butt of his revolver. He looked thickheaded, flushed, and mad.

146

Louis had a whore sitting at his table, an old woman with a beaky nose and paint on her an inch thick. She was sitting beside him with her head bent, crying down into her paint without a sound. Scared she was going to get killed.

Abe was standing in front of the bar, his arms crossed over his chest. He was enjoying himself calling Stern names.

"What in the world are you waiting for, Fatty?" he said. "I called you a pig's son and I described how your Momma got you, you comin' out of her like a turd an' all. Now what does it take for you and your lady friends here to slip your tempers?" He laughed and shook his head. "Lordy, lordy. . . and cowboys used to be as rough as cobs. Some sad comedown you three nancy-boys are. . ."

The old whore saw Lacy standing back in the dark. He saw her eyes turn toward him, and look down again right away. She made a move to get up, saw herself killed for sure, but Lacy saw Louis reach out a quick hand to take her by the arm and hold her still. Figuring the cowboys might be slow to shoot through her to him, if Abe should miss one.

Lacy looked across the room. Stern and the Australian had taken all they could take. He saw Buddy holding onto the Henry like a drowning man. Time was run out: the cowboys were going to fight.


Lacy moved out of the hall, reached back to pull the Toothpick from his belt, stepped behind Louis Bothwell and drove the knife down between his neck and collar bone as hard as he could. When the blade went in, Louis grunted and heaved to his feet—and Peter Stern must have made his play, because Abe Bothwell was shooting right that instant.

Three fast shots.

As Louis staggered away from him, reaching up to fumble with the handle of the knife, Lacy saw Stern already down. The top of his head was off and he was thrashing, leaving brains on the floor with every buck. The Australian had his pistol in his hand, and it was doing him no good. He'd made a shot and Lacy heard the bar mirror still breaking, but Abe Bothwell was smiling and shooting, not a mark on him.

Lacy drew and shot Bothwell through the hips. He fired a second time, into the gunsmoke, but missed because the man had gone down so fast. Bothwell landed hard, spun in the sawdust and fired two shots at Lacy.

It must have been a shock to him, to have a round come and strike him from where his brother was guarding, but the surprise didn't slow him up. His second round burned Lacy across the thigh and spun him half around. He heard the crack of the Henry rifle. The boy was shooting now. No more pistol shots from the Australian, though. . .

Lacy seemed to have a great deal of time to finish the half turn the bullet had knocked him into—to spin clear around and come out with the Colt's leveled where Abe Bothwell should be. Abe shot at him again and missed him clean, not smiling now, looking intent and angry from the floor. He was lying sprawled oddly, his hips broken, steadying for a better shot.

Lacy fired at his throat, and hit it. Bothwell screamed and kept screaming, all sounding muffled to Lacy ears, dulled and ringing from the gunfire. Bothwell was rolling this way and that, all fight gone. The slug must have gone clean through him, and come out at his ass.

Lacy shot at him again and blew one of his eyes out and killed him.

That fool boy was still shooting.

The Henry was cracking away, the bullets humming like bees. Lacy thought that the boy might be shooting at him, but he turned and saw that Louis Bothwell was sliding down the wall behind him, his eyes rolled white back up in his head, still plucking at the handle of the knife sticking up beside his neck. Dead, and didn't know it.

There were two red holes in his shirt where Buddy had got some shots home on him.

The shooting stopped.

Lacy called across the room. "How's Pierce?" He shouted it loud, because his ears were still ringing. His heart was going as fast as if the fight wasn't finished.

The boy didn't answer him, and he walked over through the gunsmoke to see for himself. Harry Pierce was down beside a knocked-over table, his knees drawn up to his belly. There was a puddle of blood around him, and he had his eyes squeezed shut as if he were pretending that nothing had happened to him.

Lacy felt the blood soaking his socks.

"Pierce." Lacy wished to God that that old fool Seligman Australian's shoulder. He could hear Buddy vomiting in a corner behind him. His ears were getting better.

"Pierce." Lacy wished to god that that old fool Seligman would get here. He could hear men yelling up and down the street—but none of those people had even stuck their head in the Two-bits. He looked up and saw that the old whore was gone. She must have scooted like a jackrabbit when Louis Bothwell was stabbed. Lacy reminded himself to go back over and get the toothpick back. He could see from here that Louis hadn't even drawn his revolver. Nine inches of double-edged steel pushed down into his chest. Must have taken his mind off everything else. Old Louis had needed somebody watching *his* back.

"Pierce. . ." The Australian heard him that time, and opened his eyes. "Judy?" he said. Lacy saw that he'd been shot through and through, front to back.

"She's coming. She'll be right here," Lacy said. Some long-ago girl, called for now, when it was all too late.

149

Pierce looked up at him. "Like hell," he said, and his voice sounded fine, as if nothing was wrong with him. "Like hell she'll be here." He closed his eyes again. "I was just dreaming," he said. The blood was running out of him like a fountain. Coming out in a rush at the small of his back. Lacy put his hand down there, and felt a ragged pit the size of the palm of his hand. He pressed his hand hard against that, and felt the warm pulse of the blood against his palm.

Buddy came over with vomit down his shirt and stared at Pierce.

Lacy heard people coming in the batwing door then, and turned his head to see if it was one of the deputies. But it was Seligman and a bald-headed man he hadn't seen before.

Seligman looked every year of his age when he came and knelt down beside Pierce. "Oh, dear," he said. "Oh, dear." He rolled the Australian over onto his belly, and he got blood all over the front of his suit doing that. When Pierce was rolled over, Lacy could smell the shit where his pucker-string had let loose. Seligman bent over Pierce and listened to his chest, and then tore open his shirt to get at the wounds. The old man had blood on the side of his face and his ear where he had listened to Pierce's chest.

It was all no use. Sometime in all this there was no Pierce left. Just a dead thing.

"This poor son-of-a-bitch came a long way to die," Lacy said. "All the way from God-damned Australia . . ." He felt angry at Buddy Manugian for making the Australian hit him the way he had, just to try and keep him out of the fight.

Lacy helped Seligman get up off his knees and out of the blood. "This is very bad," the old man said. "This is very bad." He seemed confused and started to kneel down again beside Pete Stern, but there was no use in that. "He's dead, Doc. All the others are dead." Lacy thought that Bristolton needed a younger doctor. "Bud," he said, "go behind the bar and get the Doc a drink."

"Yes," the old man said. "Heaven knows I could use it." He found a chair and sat down in it. "Jesus H. Christ, Lacy—how much of this is your doing?"

"The Bothwells," Lacy said. "Bud helped with Louis." Buddy came back from behind the bar with a bottle of rye whiskey. He looked as poorly as Dr. Seligman. The whole room smelled of gunsmoke and shit and blood. Lacy sat down in a chair beside Seligman and pulled off his socks. They were thick red, clotted with blood. He pulled them off and threw them away.

Then he got up and walked over to tug his knife out of Louis Bothwell.

"Jesus H. Christ," Seligman said, "don't let Dunn or Otto Manstein catch sight of that knife; the Committee'll string you up high as Haman. Sticking somebody like that. They consider that a Mexican trick, doing a man with a knife that way."

"Who's Dunn?"

"The man who was with me," Seligman said. The bald-headed man had gone, gone to get his friends, likely. "Put that damn knife away, dammit!" He uncapped the rye and took a swig.

Lacy cleaned the Toothpick on his trousers, and he got as much blood on the blade as he got off; then he slid the knife back into his gunbelt. He heard men coming, talking until they were just outside the Two-bits, then falling silent.

Must be Mister Dunn's Committee come to call. And Manstein, too. Lacy hoped the squarehead didn't hold any grudge for the ride he'd given him on buying that crow-bait.

"This is a hell of a thing," old Seligman said, sitting and looking around the room. "A hell of a thing."

The batwing doors swung open, and six men came in with shotguns. A shadow fell across a table, and Lacy looked up and saw a man standing outsie the window near him. The man stared at Lacy. He looked like a clerk, but he had a rifle in his hands.

# CHAPTER SEVENTEEN

Nobody had stolen his boots after all.

Lacy had said a polite "Good day" to the vigilance committee, gone out back to get his boots, and walked down to Miss Maynard's, people whispering along behind him all the way. Whispering along, but staying well back, most of them.

He felt sick. Not at the shooting. At the sameness of the damn trouble. The rotten *sameness* of it. Mister Gunman and his fine Bisley Colt's.

He should have let that Armenian boy go to hell on his own hook.

Manstein and the rest of the shopkeepers with their shotguns and carbines, had given Lacy some hard looks when they'd seen what a slaughter-house the Two-bits had turned into; but after all, everybody had known what the Bothwells were, and old Seligman stood up for Lacy as a decent enough fellow who'd just gotten drawn into the fight when he saw poor cowboys being shot down in cold blood. Seligman had made more of a fuss, too, about the bullet-burn across Lacy's thigh than that warranted, but it had all served to cool down the vigilance committee. Manstein had certainly remembered Lacy for all that horse-trading hoo-rah, but he hadn't taken the opportunity of pushing it.

Lucky, in fact, to have gotten off without trouble. Seligman, and Buddy being just a kid, and a good word from from the shopkeeper's brother, Norris—from the time Lacy'd bought the base-ball bat—had helped to make the difference.

"But," old Seligman said, "were I you, Lacy, I'd step somewhat lightly around Bristolton for the time being." He'd paused to tuck a pinch of stuff under his lip. "A word to the wise."

Good advice. A four-killing fight would be heard about all over Texas in the next few weeks. Good reason to get up and go while the getting was good. Any more trouble—and the Central Cattle Company wouldn't be likely to let it rest that two of their hard cases had been shot to pieces. Any more trouble, and the Rangers would be bound to send a man. . .

Another night, maybe two, of poker—men would come and play, just to say that they'd played with him—just another one or two nights, and he'd be flush to travel. No doubt they'd come to play with him, now that he'd killed two men.

A killer was a celebrity.

A man came up to him on South Street, all huffing and puffing with the news, and made to talk to Lacy about it. Congratulations, by the grin on his face. Anyone who'd been frightened of the Bothwells—maybe had Abe make a joke of them, or back them down—any of these men would stand Lacy a drink, and be pleased to do it.

The man came up and offered his hand, and opened his mouth to speak his piece. "Stand out of my way, damn you!'' Lacy said. And back the fellow went as if someone had pulled his string.

Lacy felt worse about this shooting than he'd expected. He'd often felt low after a killing, but not quite like this—this sad, tired feeling. Probably it was seeing Pete Stern and Harry Pierce go down. They'd made the best try they could, but they were out of their class. That's all there was to it.

He could have started shooting from that hallway door, shot Louis in the back, or gone for Abe first, and then got Louis as he turned. Should have opened the ball, himself. That way, the cowboys would have had a good chance of coming out of it.

*Could have, would have, might have, should have.*

It could drive a man mad, thinking like that. Thinking that living and dying were so so damn accidental.

A woman with a shopping-basket on her arm stood looking at him as he walked past, just a block from Miss Maynard's, now. He'd be damn glad to get inside there, away from these people. The woman was staring at the blood crusted down the front of his clothes; she had her hand over her mouth.

He'd be damn glad to get inside.

When the school let out, there'd be kids hanging around Miss Maynard's. They'd be wanting a look at him.

A peep at a killer, is what they'd want.

The God-damned deputies had never even *showed* at the Two-bits. Not even when it was all over. God-damned cowardly dogs.


Sarah answered the door at Miss Maynard's, and let him in without saying a word. It was a relief to be in the house, to be back with people in the life, who knew all about trouble, and didn't bone a man about something that was over and done.

Miss Maynard came rustling out of her parlor with her sampler in her hand. She looked at Lacy, but she didn't say anything either. He was glad the blood was dry enough not to be dripping on her carpets.

"Oh, Lacy, you come upstairs." Silky was hanging over the bannister, looking down at him with tears in her eyes.

When she'd got him upstairs, and peeled the bloody shirt and trousers off him, and sponged him clean with a basin of hot water, she was still teary and sniffling.

"Stop that damn crying, will you. You've got nothing to cry about."

"Oh, yes I have," she said, and wiped her nose with the back of her hand. She was untying the bandage Seligman had put on his leg.

"Leave that alone. The doctor knew what he was doing. And it's nothing much, anyway."

"You'll be riding out now; isn't that right?" she said.

"In a day or two."

She took a corner of linen rag, and set to cleaning the bullet burn as if Seligman hadn't touched it, using hot water, and enough soap to make it smart considerable.

She cleaned it, and bandaged it again with a torn strip of laundered sheet. "I told you there was nothing to that," Lacy said, "Seligman already fixed it up."

"Oh, be quiet," she said, and tied off the bandage pretty hard. Then she blew her nose on a handkerchief with a rose embroidered on the corner, and sat for a minute, looking out the window, and didn't say anything more.

She woke him in the middle of the night, kissing and hugging him. He was glad to wake; he'd been dreaming of a girl who was dead. A girl who'd been dead for a long time.

Silky lay beside him in the dark, hugging him, whispering in his ear. It made him uncomfortable; it made the dream seem real, as if this girl were the other girl, who liked him, loved him.

"Let me get some sleep, honey," he said to her. "My leg's aching some." After a moment, Silky took her arms from around him and turned away onto her side.

Lacy lay looking into the darkness. The moon was down, only faint starlight glowed at the window. He imagined for a moment that there had been no fight. That Abe Bothwell had been told to stay away from the Angle Iron people. That he himself had gone the other way, walked the other way on Main, and never even seen those cowboys fighting in the street.

Walked the other way. . .

Years too late to walk the other way. Too late the day he'd had a fist-fight with Charley Harris. . . and they'd talked themselves madder. . . and Charley went to his brother's house to get a pistol.

Could have walked the other way then. And left Charley Harris calling him a coward. And what difference would it have made?

Damn all! No difference in the world.

And Charley Harris wouldn't have been shot through the head like a foaming dog. . . and his brother, too.

That was a day Lacy remembered, morning to night. Even remembered what he'd had for breakfast: Mister Rolquist's pork sausages and cornmeal mush.

Working for the Butterfield-Kansas stage line; ostling teams for the Concords wheeling in and out. Just forty miles from Wichita. Seventeen years old and pleased as punch to be doing a man's job.

Then Charley Harris went and got his brother's pistol. And his brother Albert came back with him and dealt himself in. Might all have ended in talk, except for that damnfool Albert, a grown man with no teeth and about as many brains.

Five minutes later, Charley Harris was dead, and so was his foolish brother Albert. And Rodger Franklin Leslie— aged seventeen and a bit—was the talk of Kansas. *A dire man killer and premier pistolero*, or so the news-papers said.

From that day on, it was all high, wide, and handsome. Rushing the life from Wichita to San Francisco, with a side trip to New Orleans for Sullivan's big fight. (Met Jesse James down there, looking like a hardware merchant in a yellow plaid suit.) All good days. And killings coming fresh every year. Fools coming at him all the time. And he'd welcomed most of them; never thought twice about inviting some dirty bruiser outside a bar and blowing his brains out.

No trick to it at all. Not when you're that fast, that fine with a revolver.

No trick to it at all. And a house full of whores screwing in the cash. High-stake poker, bouncing girls, and some ladies, too, opera in San Francisco, champagne with a peach in it.

Nothing there to discourage a young buck. Everything to encourage him, in fact.

And knowing, as well, that those were prime times; high-rolling times west of the Mississippi, with Englishmen and Frenchmen, and foreigners of all kinds pouring in to see the show. To see the last fine open country before it went, to see the Indians, the buffalo, before they went, to see and taste and smell the wildest, sweetest style of living this earth could afford—before it went.

And what a devil with a gun that young Leslie was, and a fair enough devil without it. And everybody knew his name, with Thompson's, and Segrue's, and Hardin's, and

Holliday's, and Bonney's, and Ringgold's, and the Earps.

What a time that was!

Talk about Buckskin Frank Leslie, you were talking about pure hell on wheels. That boy, that young Frank Leslie, he would have strolled right through the *front* door of that saloon. Would have strolled right in and braced the Bothwells to their faces. Would have called them, given them the edge to draw—and then put them down, one and two, before ever they finished their moves at all.

Not any more.

"What are you laughing about, Lacy?" Soft, sleepy voice.

"Nothing, Little Bit, nothing at all. You go back to sleep."


Sarah came into the kitchen in the morning, to tell Lacy that Miss Maynard wanted to see him in the parlor. He finished his eggs, got up, and went on down the hall. Breakfast hadn't been much, anyway. Nothing wrong with the food, but the girls were something subdued. Nobody had much to say while Lacy was at the table.

It was no joy to be the scarfaced rough in a kitchen full of girls. Gray in his hair. These were class whores; not used to eating breakfast with knifers and shooters. Silky was cool to him, too. Passed the damson jam nicely enough, but gave him no pinches on the butt for breakfast. The other women glanced at him from time to time, as if they were afraid he'd lose his temper and turn into a grizzly bear, right at their table. A handsome young dandy, they might have been pleased enough with, killings or not; a scarface drifter, though, whose blood-crusted trousers stood up by themselves out beside the wash-tub, was not quite such a fellow of romance.

They smelled the death on him, and tiredness.

Miss Maynard nodded him to a chair in the parlor. She stared at him for a moment, then lowered her head to her sampler. Her white, withered little hands did deft stitches. She looked to be a considerable needle-woman.

"Do you intend to play any longer with the clients, Mister Lacy?" she said, not looking up at him, still sewing away.

"Another night. . . maybe two, I thought."

"People will be coming in now, more of them."

"Yes, they will, Miss Maynard."

"It would be possible, I suppose, to increase your share."

"Just another one or two nights, Miss Maynard."

She sighed, and put down her sewing. Rocking back and forth, staring at him out of her little, wrinkled, monkey's face.

"Too bad," she said, and she meant too bad about everything.

"Yes." He got up to go.

When he was at the parlor door, she said, "Mister Talbot spoke to Louis Bothwell yesterday, in private."

"In private." But not private enough. So the lawyer was more than a purchasing agent for the Cattle Company. Passed on their orders, too. Did them favors, like slipping the leash off their fighting dogs.

"I see," he said. Miss Maynard was back to her sewing, and Lacy walked out of the parlor and down the hall. Talbot was something to think about.

# CHAPTER EIGHTEEN

The girls eased up after a while and got used to him again, and sat with Lacy in the back parlor while he put some polish on his boots and buffed them up to a shine. Not easy, with the leather so cracked and worn. If he had time enough, and cash to spare, might be worthwhile to get a pair made in town. No, it wouldn't. No use getting boots made in Texas when he could have better built for half the price in Sonora.

The girls sat around the parlor, tatting, or sewing hems up or down. One, the fat one, was strumming away on the piano, and not badly either. Operetta music. When she got going strong on it, two of the girls got up and danced. Sweet on each other, the way a lot of house girls get.

For a while, nobody mentioned the shootings, then a slim girl named Agatha said it served Louis Bothwell right for trying to hide behind a woman's skirts. It seemed that the old whore from the Two-bits had been telling her tale all over town, and referring to Lacy as a Knight of the Round Table, at least. Likely, that nonsense had eased the girls as far as this particular roughneck was concerned. Silky Perkins

161

thawed, too, over her anger at last night, and asked Lacy to step out in his new-shined boots and dance with her. So he did.

They danced a two-step, and then a German waltz, spinning around around the parlor with the two Boudiccas as fine as new-mint money. It became a contest, to see which couple could do the neatest steps, and Lacy and Silky and the two lover-girls put on a considerable show. One of the girls, a fine, big girl named Clarise, with upswept hair black and thick as a horse's mane, was a particularly good dancer. She didn't appear to mind her steps in the least, but tripped and whirled around the room like a professional. Her lover, a little carrot-haired girl with freckles, wasn't nearly so good, but did keep up. Even so, Lacy and Silky Perkins might have won; he was a fair dancer, and she was better than fair, but Silky spoiled their chances by fooling, kissing him and making faces. The girls laughed, but when the waltz was over, they applauded more for the black-haired girl and her friend.

The prize was a bunch of blue-bells that Mrs. Collins brought in from a big bunch in the kitchen.

At dinner, everything was easy. Miss Maynard came into the kitchen to eat, something she usually didn't do, and they had deep-fried chicken, gravy and biscuits, and green peas. Peach pie for dessert. Some of the girls talked about sending a boy to the parlor on Main Street for ice cream, but they didn't.

After dinner, Lacy took Silky Perkins out for a walk. It was late afternoon, cooler than it had been, and they walked out back toward the river bed. There were some boys hanging around the street at the front of the house, trying to get a look at Lacy, probably. Not as many as there had been, but still a few.

Lacy walked out with her through the soft green sagebrush, all the way to the bank of the river. The brush tugged at Silky's skirt as they walked, so that she had to hold it gathered up in one hand, off the ground. Flocks of birds were wheeling up from the cottonwoods across the river.

They stood on the bank, looking down into the deep, white, pebbled streambed as if a real river was still running down it, ripples, gurgling, fish and all.

It was pretty, even without the water; the cottonwoods grew thick along the bank; and their long branches bent down along the gully on either side to make a canopy of light-green little leaves. They were big cottonwoods.

"If the river was runnin', we could go in swimmin'," Silky said. "Why don't you stay the week out, anyway? People in town don't care that you shot the Bothwells. They're glad of it, most of them. Except Mary Lincoln, maybe."

"Who's Mary Lincoln?"

"Oh," Silky said, "she's just a nigger girl Abe Bothwell used to go with." She laughed. "They were real sweethearts. Mary used to say he was goin' to marry her. Do you believe that? Marry a colored girl?" She reached down and picked a sage leaf and crushed it in her fingers and smelled the perfume from it. "Smells like hot sausage," she said. "Catch me losin' my heart over a gunman like that."

"I can't stay the week, Little Bit. I'll be going tomorrow, the day after, latest."

She blushed. "I didn't mean what I said. I wasn't talkin' about you."

"I know."

He heard something behind him, way back, moving in the brush. He put his hand on the girl's arm, to be ready to push her to the ground, then he turned to look.

Two boys were standing back there, just their heads and

shoulders showing above the sage. They were a considerable way back, staring at him and the girl. They were poor-enough dressed, it looked like. Laborers' sons from out on the flats.

Lacy bent and picked up a rock and threw it. They ducked away, and both of them took off like prairie chickens, then, and ran all the way back past the side of the house. Silky had bent down to pick up rocks, too, and she was chunking them at the running kids as hard as she could, even when they were too far away to hit. "You dirty little Irish trash!" She yelled at them until they were gone out of sight. "Now, what do you think of that? Those little son-of-a-bitches are always coming around to look in the windows and get an eyefull. They're dirty Catholics, every damn one of them!"

She marched around in the sagebrush, steaming like a small locomotive, then she calmed down and came back and hugged Lacy and French-kissed him. "Nobody's lookin' now," she said.

They stood and looked down the river bed for a while longer, holding hands, then she said, "Say, Lacy. . . I guess you shot men before this, haven't you?"

"Yes," he said, "I have."

"Plenty of them, huh?"

"Yes."

She gave him a sidelong look. "In a business way?" she said. "You sure don't have to answer me."

"Sometimes, in a business way. . ."

"Well," she said. "Can I ask you something?"

"I know what you want to ask me," Lacy said. "You want to know how come a nice boy like me got into a business like that."

Silky blushed, and then threw back her head and laughed. She had one of the nicest laughs Lacy had heard. She laughed freely and right out loud; didn't try to squeeze it down to be polite.

She caught her breath, and said, "That was it, all right!" And she was off again, laughing.

When they were walking back to the house, she said, "I wondered about it, because you don't seem so tough, you know? You're not mean with people."

Lacy laughed. "Hell, I'm just old and tired. I used to be mean as a snake."

"I don't believe that," Silky said. "I think that you're a real gentleman."

"No," he said, "I'm not."

Upstairs, in bed in her room, Silky re-bandaged the bullet-burn on his leg, then she wouldn't give him his pants back. She lay across the bed in her dress. "—I'm wrinkling this dress to pieces . . ." And she pulled his drawers down and lay there feeling his cock and playing with it. Then she began to suck at it, red in the face and her eyes closed.

"I love you," she said, when they were finished.


The lawyer, Talbot, didn't come to the house that night, but a hell of a crowd of men did. To see the new Bill Hickok, apparently, and happy enough to play a few hands of poker with him, too. Seemed that if Lacy could just kill a couple of men a week, he might make a very good thing out of playing poker with the gawks.

Why not?

Earp used to make money dealing after a shooting, so did Hickok, come to that.

So had Buckskin Frank Leslie, in his day.

Miss Maynard was very pleased. And so she should be, because Lacy was playing very well, his professional hand coming back to him, and the marks seemed as pleased with losing as with winning, as long as they could sit down at the table with him.

These men would sit and play, and eat sandwiches and

165

drink some whiskey, and smoke a couple of Miss Maynard's fine Cuban cigars, and play out their hands, and lose. Then—with every appearance of being satisfied—they joked and laughed and got up and strolled around the parlor, stole glances down at Lacy's Bisley-model .45, and sometimes picked a girl and took her upstairs.

Being so long out of the whorehouse line, Lacy found himself surprised anew at how odd men were, in company of this kind. "Half beast, half boy," a madam had once said to him. "That's what men are." Hard to say that wasn't true.

Hell, it was true.

By the early hours, he was ahead four hundred dollars, and had a promissory note from a man named Beeson for eighty dollars more. It had been small-stake play, but they'd kept coming.

Up over a thousand dollars now, even with Miss Maynard's cut, but the people were bothering him. After supper, a couple of drummers had asked him about the fight, wanted to know all about it, sorry they'd missed it, had seen Harry Tracy kill a man in Wyoming, and so on and on. It was no pleasure, and Lacy came close to losing his temper with them. Silky had come in just then, with a horse rancher on her arm—just come back downstairs—had seen Lacy stiffening-up at the two drummers, and came over to talk them into the back parlor to meet some girls.

Another man, later, had tried to start talking about pistols with Lacy, but he was a smarter man and soon saw that Lacy didn't like the subject, and changed it to hunting javalinas. Lacy was happy enough to talk about that, though his experience had been that cooking javalinas was a lot more trouble than hunting them.

The night had gone on like that straight through, hour after hour, with men peeping at him, and nudging at him, and mentioning this or that about the Bothwells, and offering him drinks.

It was like the shootings, in a way. Not so bad in itself, as just. . .tiring, sickening by being so familiar. If he had seen one goggle-eyed drunk yellow-belly come nudging up to him in a saloon or whorehouse, talking about a shooting or a knifing or this badman or that, he had seen a hundred.

There were some years, way back when, that he'd enjoyed that sort of attention. Been real fond of it, young jackass that he'd been. Having a party of loafers around you to play you up and buy your beers, and ask if they could handle the Colts.

Some considerable years back, he'd liked that sort of thing. Thought it real prime, when it started.

But tonight, it was no pleasure. A danger, too, of course. If Jeff Compton could recognize him years later and the mustache shaved (and now with this damned scar across his face), then others could as well. It would be information the Rangers might like to hear. The Bristolton vigilance committee would be interested too. What he'd gotten away with as a tough drifter up against a pair of known Texican gunmen, he damn well might not get away with as Buckskin Frank Leslie.

Lacy had seen that sort of thing happen to men with big reputations. Hell, it had happened to him, and more than once. So, all this gathering-round might put poker money into his pocket, but it might put trouble into his pocket, too. More trouble than he could handle.


By three in the morning, Lacy was feeling as if he'd been thrown and dragged, and people were still coming into Miss Maynard's looking for a raree-show and a piece of ass at once. Lacy was stuffed full of roast chicken sandwiches and beer, and he had over two-thousand dollars in his kick. And he'd had enough.

"Gents, another few hands and I'm out."

The men at the table gave the usual grumbles and mumbles, though since they were, most of them, losing as much of their shirts as penny ante would allow, Lacy didn't see it as worth paying attention to. Something else, as well; if this fuss about the shooting kept on for a few more days, likely some damn fool would get drunk and call him out. That was something he didn't need at all.

"Sorry boys, I'm beat right down to the ground. You folks play mighty hard-nosed poker!" That got some chuckles out of them. They were glad to think of themselves as cruel high-rollers. It occured to Lacy, not for the first time, that the whores had to put up with this sort of shit and worse. The notion of not just having to jolly these duck-walkers along, but to lie down on a bed as well for a fat-bellied hump; well, that was a pretty grim notion.

He was dealing out a hand, "Next to last, boys," when Sarah, toting a tray of empty beer glasses past the table, paused to mutter to him that there was trouble at the door. Miss Maynard must have sent her through to him.

"Got to go out back," he said, and stood up. Last thing he wanted was a big music-hall audience if he had to hit some drunk cowpoker west. "Mister Sanders," this to a skinny young ribbon-clerk who'd been hanging around all night, "do me the favor of playing out my hand, if you please."

Mister Sanders was very pleased to do it, and sat down in Lacy's chair with a flourish. Lacy walked off in the firm assurance that Mister Sanders was going to lose his ante for him.

He went out into the hall, and saw Miss Maynard standing by the front door, looking angry as a wet hen. She beckoned to him.

"You go on out there, Mister Lacy. That person considers himself too good, if you can believe it, to enter this house!"

Lacy slipped the keeper-loop off the Bisley, stepped past her, and swung the door open.

There was nobody on the porch.

"Well sir, do you intend to come down here and speak with me, or must I set fire to this nest of whores and hypocrites to winkle you out!" The voice was a fair bellow: Lacy could hear it echoing off the buildings on the other side of South Street.

Mister Meager was standing in the middle of the walk, his rusty stovepipe hat tilted well back on his head. His empty left sleeve was tucked down into his trousers, and his beard shone silver in the moonlight. He looked big as a horse.

"And you, Eleanor Maynard!" he roared out. "You damned old salt mackerel! Stop your peeping and shut that door!"

Lacy heard Miss Maynard let out an angry cluck, and the door slammed shut. He went on down the steps to the walk. The Angle Iron foreman loomed on the walk, waiting for him.

"Good morning, sir."

Meager put out a shovel-sized hand and crushed Lacy's a little. "Good morning, son." The old man stood looking down at him for a moment. "Pardon me for shouting you out of there like that, but the fact is Eleanor Maynard and I haven't suited for some years now. Not since '53, in fact."

"I see," Lacy said.

"No, you don't. No reason you should. Fact is, I was married to her sister, a lady who was an angel, mind you, and who had nothing but pain and grief from Eleanor." He mumbled something, and hitched the big Walker Colt higher on his waist. "None of your business, of course. Shouldn't have mentioned it."

"What can I do for you, Mister Meager?"

169

"Well, now," Meager said. "For the first, I'd like to thank you for stepping in to help my men in that fight with the Bothwell scum. I'm sure they would have murdered the boy, too, if you hadn't thrown your hat in."

"No need for thanks, Mister Meager."

The old man glared at him. "The hell there isn't! And I'm damn well giving them to you!" Then he sighed, and said, "Now, there is another thing, Lacy."

"Sir?"

"I'm here to ask you if you'd consider riding for Angle Iron in that horse drive. We. . ." he champed his jaws like an old plowhorse, "we are having some difficulty getting men to replace the two fellows those scum shot down."

Mister Meager looked old and tired in the moonlight.

# CHAPTER NINETEEN

Lacy woke before dawn.

Dark and cool, the window curtains stirring in a breeze. Pitch dark outside the window. Silky turned and murmured in her sleep.

Lacy should have been tired. He'd been weary enough two, three hours ago, when they'd gone to bed. But he felt awake, now, fresh and strong.

He slid out of bed and walked across the room to the wardrobe, the floorboards cool against his bare feet. He found his clothes in the dark, dressed quietly. They'd get along well enough without him. That morning, Big William had been up and sitting out on the back porch, sipping soup, still looking a shade more gray than black, but coming along. He'd be working in another day or so.

Silky had said goodbye before they went to sleep. She hadn't hung on him at all, just wished him luck, bit his ear, ridden him like a pony, and gone off to sleep. A fine girl.

He finished dressing, and carried his boots and hat to the bed. Reached up and slid his gunbelt off the bed post, then bent and kissed the sleeping girl in among the soft curls at the base of her neck.

He closed the room door behind him, and went quietly in his stocking feet down the narrow corridor. The walls glowed dim red from the night lamp at the head of the stairs. Behind him, as he went, he heard a girl crying softly in one of the rooms. Hard to walk through a whorehouse at dawn and not hear that.

Old man Meager was waiting out on South Street in the gray light before dawn, standing like a white-bearded statue—holding two horses: his own big roan, and Harry Pierce's sorrel. What was that horse's name? Tiger.

Lacy lugged his saddle, bed-roll, and booted rifle down the walk—Mrs. Collins had already been up and doing when he'd gone to the storeroom to get it, and said "Good morning" to the old man. Meager nodded, and watched Lacy saddle-up. The sorrel tried to hold its breath, but Lacy kneed it out of him and cinched up tight.

"I suppose," Meager said, "you'll regret leaving the sporting life."

"No," Lacy said, "not with those bug-eyes hanging around, talking about the fight."

"Trash," the old man said, and he heaved himself up onto the roan—the big horse grunted when it took his weight—turned the animal, and led the way west, up South Street toward the old riverbed, and out of Bristolton.


The sun came up when they rode out onto the prairie; it came up blazing and fiery red. Meager tilted his stovepipe hat so the brim would shade his eyes, and turned in his saddle to talk to Lacy. His white beard was red with the rising sun; looked like it was burning.

"You eat before you come out?"

"Not hungry."

"Good. Can't stand a man that always has to be gobbling

172

at food.'' The old man faced front in his saddle, and kicked the big roan into a lope.

They rode into deep grass, the old man leading, avoiding the ridge the wagon road ran on. They cut straight off into the country, scaring up skylarks and prairie hens, clouds of sleepy grasshoppers from under their horses' hooves.

Lacy turned from time to time to look behind them, as much for the possibility of stray Comanche bucks off hunting, as any chase by the Central Cattle Company. It would take a while for those people in Chicago or Amarillo or wherever to chew over and digest the news Talbot must have sent them about the Bothwells. It occured to Lacy that they wouldn't be much pleased with Talbot about losing their people.

So, it was Comanches he thought might be trouble, if there was to be trouble.

''Are you a nervous man, Lacy?'' the old man said, still riding ahead. He'd raised his voice rather than turning his head.

''No.''

''Then why in blazes are you dancing around in your saddle, sir? Damn it, I can't bear a man who can't sit still and ride.''

The old man had Lacy over a barrel for a moment, then he realized that Meager must have seen his shadow shifting, where the rising sun threw it far along the grass.

''I understand that the Comanches hunt through here.''

Meager turned in his saddle and glared back at him. ''The Comanche? Mister Lacy, I know every single Antelope Indian in this part of the country. Snake, Hawk, and Spider clan as well. Every damned one! I know Mister Parker well, and in fact put a bullet through his leg when the red-haired son-of-a-bitch was still a boy. So, you will do me the favor of sitting still in your saddle, and not be jumping about like a girl at the Governor's Cotillion! I'll tell you, sir, if there is any Comanche, or Kiowa either, close enough to trade beadwork for a bite of snuff!''

"Yes, sir," Lacy said.

It looked to be a long ride.

But if he'd figured the old man for a sour traveler, he'd been mistaken. Not long after his Indian speech—Lacy was to learn that old Meager had a speech for almost any subject—the old man's voice rumbled out in a song, bellowed without any warm-up preliminaries. After a verse or two, Lacy identified the song as *Just Before The Battle, Mother*, and seeing no need to be shy, in fact suspecting the old man wouldn't like it if he was, he raised his own voice in song, trying to match Meager in volume, if not in style. The old man was a very sentimental singer, and threw in sobs and groans wherever the sentiments were called for.

It was a considerable performance, and might well have earned the Angle Iron foreman free beers, and maybe a fair living, if he'd turned professional and toured the mining camps set too high in the mountains for the professionals to visit. When he sang, Lacy could hear the Irish in him, under the Texican.

After *Just Before The Battle, Mother*, they sang *Jim Crow*, and *Fair Stood The Wind For France*.


By near to midday, they were on Angle Iron range. The very first stretch of fence they met had been cut.

"God damn it to hell!" the old man roared, and he swung off his horse tugging a wire-hammer from the back pocket of his trousers. He carried his suit jacket neatly folded across his saddlebow, as though he might meet a lady at any moment and have to put it on without delay. "Those cowardly dogs have cut it to bits!" And he commenced to

174

tug and heave at the loose-coiled wire to work out a length enough to tack onto the posts.

Lacy got down after a quick look around while the old man was busy wrestling with the wire. It would have been a reasonable place for a rifleman to wait for somebody to dismount to fix the fence. But the only parcel of brush for miles was skimpy, with no man or no horse showing, and the short-grass on this stretch wouldn't have hidden a child.

Between them, they got two strands tacked-up well enough to serve, and Lacy got a smart cut across his hand, doing it. "Don't care for that wire, do you, boy?" Meager said.

"Not much."

"Well, that's all you know," the old man said. "If you were in the cattle business, you'd know what a blessing that Glidden wire is! Hell, without it, there wouldn't *be* any damned cattle business!"

Lacy muttered something about free range, and climbed back onto Harry Pierce's horse.

"Free range!" the old man snorted, hauling himself up onto the roan. "You sound like some damn fool horse rancher—if that." He kicked the roan out into a lope, and Lacy fell in behind him. Meager went on talking—shouting, rather—facing straight ahead. "*Free range. . . only people who talk about free range as if it was white cake and sugar icing never knew the cattle business when it *was* all free range. Damndest mess you ever saw. Every thieving tinhorn trying to run his cattle in with yours, branding-over, mavericking every beast that walked or ran. *Free range*. Free enough if you cared to hang a man for every section of it. Vile greed and dire dumbness, is more the way of it." He subsided for a moment to turn his roan down a grassy slope to a bare wash beyond. There was a gather of cattle grazing beyond the wash. Longhorn, with English blood already bred through them. Fair-looking stock. Better than fair. Breeder heifers, looked like.

"There's our foundation for next year's herd," Meager said. "A piece of it, anyway." He sat his horse, looking out over the herd with some satisfaction. "Lot of strength in there. Lot of good beef." He turned his roan away. "I have no patience with talk about the old days in this business. I say old days were bad days. Except for the people, of course. Good people in those days. Men *and* women were better human beings than you'll ever find, now. Better every way. All trash, nowadays." He flashed Lacy a glance. "Present company excepted, of course."

They reached headquarters in early afternoon, just as they finished the last verse and chorus of *'Mid Shot And Shell, I Am Dreaming Of My Own Bluebell*.

Old Rudy Snell and Wry-Neck Tom Clark came riding out to meet them with rifles across their saddlebows. Lacy was stuck again by the poor quality of men Angle Iron was stuck with. A few young, tough, tearing boys might have made the difference in persuading the cattle company to let this ranch alone. God knows Texas wasn't short of boys who liked to fight. Could be the ranch was just too far out in the lonesome. The bigger outfits down by the Bravo would be having first dibs on fine young cow-pushers.

"How-do, boss."

"Tom," Meager said, "Mister Lacy is joining us to work our horse drive." Old Snell gave Lacy a wink. "You men see he's settled. And, Lacy, you may use that pony if you wish, and rope out two more from the remuda for your string."

"Yes, sir."

"And keep in mind that we treat stock gently on this

176

outfit. I'll have no running a horse for no reason, nor abusing an animal, either.''

''No, sir.''

Meager grunted, gave his roan enough kick to make it grunt, and rode off toward the ranch house.

''Well, well,'' Snell said, ''I expected to see you honorary marshal of the town, Lacy, considering you done those Bothwells like you did!''

''That's right,'' Clark said, and nodded as well as his twisted neck allowed.

''I was lucky,'' Lacy said. ''Nothing more too it than that.''

''Do tell?. . .'' Snell said as the three of them rode to the far corral. ''Lucky against one of those boys, I will allow. Lucky against the both of them's a harder plug to chew.''

''True, just the same.''

''Hear Louis didn't get off no shots at all,'' Clark said.

Lacy didn't say anything.

Clark gave his him a glance, ''I'm sure glad they're gone, though. I will say that.''

''No trouble on *this* horse drive,'' old Snell said.

Lacy didn't say anything.


The other men treated him the same way, when he brought his roll into the bunkhouse. They treated him like a hard case, but a hard case on their side, and one who'd saved them a lot of trouble. None of them, except Bud Manugian, mentioned Pete Stern or Harry Pierce.

''I know Harry was my friend,'' Bud said to Lacy when they went over to the cook shed. ''He was just tryin' to keep me out of it.'' Bud looked up at Lacy as they walked. ''I suppose Mister Meager is payin' you a lot to come out and shotgun the drive. I guess a person like you don't spend much time just tending stock.''

"I'll be getting what the other drovers will earn on the drive, Bud. I'm just out here to lend a hand.''

"Is that so? Well, I'd thought they'd pay more just to have you out here.''

"Mister Meager isn't paying me to murder people, Bud.''

The boy's face flushed red. "I beg your pardon, Mister Lacy; I sure didn't mean any such thing.''

"Good evening.'' Louise Bristol was standing beside the long plank table, smiling.

"Good evening, Ma'am,'' Lacy said, and Buddy ducked his head and said the same. Old Meager came rumbling over to seat her at the head of the table, and the other hands clustered 'round, jostling for space on the side benches.

Lacy sat one down from the head of the table, with Buddy between him and Miss Bristol.

"Mister Meager tells me that you'll join him on our horse drive after all, Mister Lacy. I'm very pleased.''

"My pleasure, Ma'am.''

Meager cleared his throat loudly at the other end of the table, and the men quieted down.

"Dear God, we appreciate your generous provision of this food, and'' —he paused to glare at a cowboy named Gifford, who was giggling like a fool over something a friend of his had just said—"*and* will try to be worthy of these vittles by not acting like jackasses!'' Gifford straightened up.

Manuel started thumping the big, chipped platters down on the table; boiled potatoes, beef stew with chili-peppers in it, biscuits, red beans and gravy, and pecan pie for dessert. It all hit the table at once, and some reached for it just as fast, but Meager barked them back, and then personally served out a plate to be passed down to Miss Louise. Then the men fell to.

"Biscuits, Ma'am?" Lacy passed her the plate.

She took one, and broke and buttered it. "I . . . I owe you our thanks, Mister Lacy. . . for what you did, in town. It was very brave."

She kept looking down, buttering the biscuit.

"It was an unpleasant thing to happen, Miss Louise. No need to mention it." Poor lady. Her looks couldn't have been much to start with, and all this trouble sure hadn't helped. She looked tired-out, homely as a kitchen table.

Bud and the other hands sitting close-by were all ears.

"Well, I thank you, anyway," she said. She finished buttering the biscuit, and set it down carefully on the edge of her plate. "It is a wonderful thing," she said, "to be in the midst of trouble. . . and find a friend."

# CHAPTER TWENTY

The next four days were all work. Dawn-to-dark work—and sometimes before dawn and after dark work. Getting in shape for the drive, gathering in the cattle so a short crew could watch them better, building two new corrals for the horses due in, and furbishing ropes and reins, halters and head-stalls, and all the tackle from the stable and farrier's shack.

Lacy found himself respecting the Angle Iron hands considerably more than he had. As fighters they were likely nothing much, not a fierce bunch at all, but as working busted-finger cowpokers, they were good as any, and better than most. He hadn't sweated out such a river since he was a boy working on the farm. Earning a living. That's what folks called it.

It was a strong-strap cinch that saloon-shootings, guiding hunters, pimping, card-playing and even lying in bed with Silky Perkins just didn't match it for effort required.

Lacy soaked his hands to ease the blisters, slept like a chunk of rock, and ate One-eye Manuel's cooking in three-pound portions.

He was happier than he'd been in some time.

Miss Louise came out and worked alongside them in the stable and tackle-room, sorting harness, sewing, stripping, and oiling the leathers. It was hard hand-work, but she didn't shirk it. She was shy, but a good-natured woman, and always concerned about the men. It seemed a shame, to Lacy, that the woman was so plain, bony as a cart-mare, the way she was.

They were to pull out the morning of the fifth day, and they did, but it took some doing. Lacy got up that morning, his back stiff as a board, ate a fast breakfast in the dark—not much joshing or horseplay at three o'clock in the morning—and then worked the soreness out of his back in loading the chuck wagon with hundred-pound bean sacks, and a two-hundred pound pit-cooked side of beef. The beef was courtesy of Miss Louise, who had fancy ideas of feeding drovers.

By the time the beans and beef and flour and salt and pork and belly-meat and doctoring chest and spare lariat line and a sack of horseshoes and nails and tools and bedrolls were all loaded, there was nothing more for Lacy to do than gather a few more sacks of dry cowshit and brittle brush for cook-fire tinder, in case they camped out far in the grass. And that was all he had to do before sun-up, except carry enough water buckets from the well to fill the two barrels on the wagon.

That done, he was done.

It was a relief to get on Tiger, and ride.

Nine of them were going out, more than enough to drive fifty-odd horses, no matter how rank. The extra four or five gun-riders, and, Lacy thought, would more than likely be needed. The Central Cattle Company had gone to some trouble to buy out Angle Iron: stealing their horse herd, cutting their wire, sending Talbot 'round to make his offers, and then calling on the Bothwells to do some straight-on killing. A lot of trouble. Lacy didn't expect them to stop trying now.

If they could keep Angle Iron horse-poor, they'd won the game.

The only question was when they'd hit. If it was Lacy's call, he would hit the Angle Iron people on their way down to get the horses. They wouldn't expect the trouble then, wouldn't be set for it at all.

But the Cattle Company would be business men; they'd want their profit on the deal. So, they would surely wait, raid on the return trip, and take the horses, too.

Lacy wondered who they'd send. Fighting in open country was different than pulling a revolver on a man in a barroom. It took longer thinking, and an eye for country. It was more like soldier's fighting. Lacy'd never liked rifle-work. Too easy for cold men and cowards to hide behind that distance.

But this would be rifle work, no doubt about it.

He spurred the sorrel up alongside Meager's horse. The old man was jogging along in his usual fashion, sitting his saddle as straight as a die, looking front.

"Mister Meager."

"Mister Lacy?"

"I believe they'll try for us only after we've got the horses."

"Certainly. The damn thieves!"

"Still, they might send one or two after us now, just to fire some rounds and un-settle the men."

The old man cocked an eye at him. "Weary with honest work, Mister Lacy? Tired of chores?" He smiled, (the first

182

smile Lacy had seen him accomplish) and said, "Oh, go on, you rascal—take that murdering buffalo gun you have, and scout ahead."

Lacy smiled back at him, tipped his hat, and wheeled back to let old Snell know he was riding out. Snell was playing top hand for the drive, and feeling mighty important about it.

When he'd given Snell the word, he pulled rein alongside Bud Manugian.

"Bud, you feeling all right about that shooting in town? Don't feel shy about it?"

"No, Lacy, I feel all right about that. All right, now, I guess." He looked at though he was still wondering about it, though.

"The reason I ask, is that you went to shooting in that fight, scared or not. And you hit what you shot at."

Bud looked pale at the recollection.

"Well, you did," Lacy said. "If you're up for it, I'd like you to Tail-end Charley this outfit. Take that damn no-account Henry of yours, and drop back a mile."

"Okay. I will."

"It's all right with Snell that you do it, and I'm not bothering the old man to ask him. You mind this. Any people running along behind this outfit will be looking for you to cut your throat. You understand that?"

Bud nodded.

"If they are trailing, and see you, they'll try to take you without shooting. Maybe wave to you and ride up bold as brass like any drifters looking for conversation. But you let 'em get close, they'll pull you off that pony and stick a knife into you."

"I'll look out," Buddy said.

"You see you do, boy. And don't always be riding dead

behind us, either. Scoot on off to the side for a few miles, this way and that way. You might ride onto some people weren't expecting you.''

''Okay.''

''Stay off the rises, and if you do come onto somebody, fire three fast shots. I've told Snell, and if the men hear three fast shots, they'll ride back to you, pronto. . .''

''I'll do 'er.'' Buddy was already looking extra serious and responsible.

''Go and do it, then,'' Lacy said. ''And keep looking around you like an hoot-owl, you may make it back.'' He reached over and slapped the boy on the shoulder, then kicked Tiger into a lope and started the long run out front.

The sorrel was a short-necked horse with a bucky stride, but it was strong and a stayer. Lacy rode well out of sight of the outfit, the big Sharps balanced across his saddlebow.

It felt good, after the days of close living and close working with the cowpokers, to be out front and alone for a while. It was a clear, hot day. The only clouds were a long streak of milky white against the horizon to the north. For the rest, the sky was blue as a mountain lake except where the sun rose to noon, white-hot and burning. Lacy felt the sun's heat on his shoulders, beyond the shadow of his hat-brim. The grass-flowers were out fine and bright, and the smell of crushed grass came up to him from the sorrel's hooves as he rode.

No sound but the wind—barely a breeze, at that—combing through the prairie grasses. A north wind, bringing the last of the year's coolness down from the high country a thousand miles away.

A thousand miles away. . .

From a mountain ranch beside a river. . . from a great

resort hotel resting in the Rockies like a jewel. . .

The thousand miles was nothing, to the wind.

He saw something move. Pulled the sorrel up short, and cocked the Sharps. A way away. Not a rider; maybe a riderless horse. Not buffalo. Not stock, too light and swift.

Two antelope came flowing down a rise.

They were a good way out, maybe five, six hundred yards. Too long a shot, even for the Sharps, though Lacy had known men who could have made it, from a rest. Anyway, no use shooting, now. They had meat enough with them, and no use letting off the Sharps just to be making noise.

Could be somebody listening for that kind of noise.

He didn't feel like killing one of them, anyway. Pretty things—and scrawny eating, when you came right down to it.

So the Comanches had come and gone through this section, and some game was drifting back. Not much yet. When he'd first ridden into Texas. . . 1874. . . the Panhandle country had been thick with game, buffalo still running in the draws, herds of antelope, prairie chickens all over. And yet, nothing compared to the old days, he'd heard. Old Meager would have known those days, when the buffalo came thundering like line storms, when Texicans used dried wild-turkey breasts instead of flour for their baking. Texas must have been damn near heaven, in those days. If you didn't mind the heat, and the Comanches, the Kiowa, and General Santa Anna.

And the Central Cattle Company—and all the other combinations—intended to sew this country up, once for all. Sew it up, and strap it down tight.

It would be a pleasure to bypass simple hard cases like the Bothwells, go straight to some knacky office in Amarillo and blow the brains out of the Central Cattle Company, whoever it proved to be.

185

No use in that, of course. Lay some fat fool out beside his leather-top desk in Amarillo, and it would only mean some wires sent off to Houston, and then to Chicago. And then, for all Lacy knew, New York City and London, England. The big money went back all the way.

It was best to keep it all forthright. Out of Bristolton, now, it was the guns that counted. And the men shot.

He rode up the slope of a low rise—there was no real high country till out past the Staked Plain—and pulled up below the ridge, dismounted, and carried the Sharps up for a look-see.

Nothing.

Grass. . . and grass. . . and grass. The clouds along the horizon were shading darker, stretching higher into the sky. A storm building there, a long way off. Days off. They'd be lucky to have a storm sweep through before they brought the horse herd up. Find runs without hours of searching for a wet sink. It would be a piece of luck.

Lacy sat cross-legged in the ridge grass, the big rifle across his lap, and dug in the pocket of his buckskin vest for the stub of one of Miss Maynard's Cuban cigars. He scratched a lucifer on the sole of his boot, lit up, and took some slow puffs. Wonderful tobacco, those Spanish people raised: must be that hot sun and the sea air working together in the leaves, somehow.

When he finished the cigar, he'd mount up and ride some further, way down into the flats, where the grass grew taller.

Jeff Compton'd probably finished that new vest by now; have to remember to pick that up. Funny, drawing on old Jeff like that, for all the world like a Kansas City coke-fiend. Must have been waiting to hear that name spoken sometime by somebody. Must have been afraid of that.

Maybe pick up a fancy belt, too. Jeff had some nice

tooled belts on that counter. No use going down to Mexico looking too needy. Be nice to go riding down there on that gray. *Rain*. Who'd have thought a sharper like Talbot would think to name a horse so well.

He rode into camp just after dark, and hadn't seen hide nor hair of riders. Lacy'd been worrying about the boy as the evening came on. Bud, except for old Meager, was the only one of the bunch Lacy could have trusted to stay spritely all day, trailing his bunch all alone. Still, he was young for it. Too young.

So when Lacy rode in, he was pleased to see Bud Manugian just hauling the saddle off his Blackie beside the cookwagon.

Lacy trotted the sorrel over to him, and looked a question.

"Nothing and nobody, Lacy." Bud lugged his saddle and bed-roll off to the fire-side. "Saw some antelope, and that was all."

"I saw some, too," Lacy said, and swung down off the sorrel with a grunt. "Ride back there tomorrow too, then."

"Okay."

"But mind you don't get careless. Just because you saw nobody doesn't mean that nobody saw you."

Bud nodded. "That's right," he said.

The hands were tired that night; no japes around the fire or skylarking out of the Angle Iron boys. They sang some songs—were going to sing one about a girl's gash, but old Meager wouldn't let them—prayed over their beans and beef (the old foreman was a terror for prayers), set out night guards, rolled into their soogins, and slept.

They rode three more days, and came into the yards at Clayton on the morning of the fourth. They'd seen only a peddler's wagon on the trail down. Not one other man anywhere near their track. The Cattle Company hadn't cared to bother.

# CHAPTER TWENTY-ONE

Clayton wasn't much more than a railroad spur and cattlepens. Looked to be a couple of saloons and whore-cribs down the line beside the water tank, but old Meager didn't intend to lose a day drying out drunk-sick cow-pokers, so he ordered the men to stay put, camped out of town. Lacy, to his surprise, got the old man's nod to go into Clayton for a keg of beer. "One keg. Just one, mind."

Lacy trotted the sorrel down along the pens toward the shanties clustered beside the tank. It was hot as blazes. A few miles further south and a few days made a difference in the heat; this was getting to be summer Texas weather, and no mistake.

They'd spent the hours since they'd ridden in talking with George Truckee. Truckee was shipping agent for the Texas and Southern, and he'd made the mistake of sticking around until Meager had come in for the horses. The old man had raked him hard over the stock's condition, claiming the horses hadn't been watered for the trip up from Easton, and looked to have been fed wet straw, if anything at all.

Truckee, a small fat man with a wandering eye, had taken all this calmly enough, which he could afford to do, since in fact the horses were in good shape. Fifty-three solid well-found broomtails. Not one of them could be called a first-rate dasher, but they had the look of useful ranch stock; no splints thrown out, no bowed tendons, no rales, no founders. Most appeared saddle-broke as well; which would save the wranglers considerable time and trouble.

No-one was strolling in the sunshine along the skid-road in Clayton, just two dogs nose-to-tailing beside a trashheap. There was a tar-paper barrack tacked-up for the railroad crews coming through or holding over for a night, but nothing else respectable.

A man came out of the barrack in his long underwear, to have a look as Lacy rode by. Not friendly, not unfriendly. Two passers-through, passing through.

There was a choice, regarding the keg of beer.

One shack had a fresh poorly-painted sign—limned on a square of tar-paper—of a red rooster. The other shack had harmonium music whining away inside.

Lacy chose the one with the fresh-painted sign. Thought it showed ambition.

He slid off the sorrel, left it ground-tied (trash-tied, was more like it) since there was no hitch-rail, thumbed the keeper-loop off the hammer of his Colt, and ducked through the doorway into the dark.

The smell—the stink of sour sweat and sour beer and dirty socks—was the smell of home. Lacy was surprised how much he'd missed rushing the growler in a barrel house. And this was a prime specimen.

There was a row of whiskey barrels lined up on the right—the whole place was no bigger than fifteen feet by fifteen feet—and the barrels were covered with two planks for a serving bar. There were no chairs in the shack at all, just two cobbled-up benches with three loafers weighing them down. All three were armed, but they looked a deal too drunk to find their revolvers, let alone fight with them. The barkeep was a halfbreed with a friendly smile and no teeth in it at all.

"Well now, come on in, mister!" His voice sounded strange, but you could understand him. The three loafers had nothing to say.

"Lacy leaned on the bar-planks and looked at the bottles stacked on a shelf behind. They were dirty, and looked like re-fills, most of them. "You make your own whiskey?"

"Sure-do!"

Bad news.

"You carry railroad whiskey?"

"Why sure, but that'd cost you a lot more than mine."

"I'll have a shot of the railroad juice."

The bar-keeper pouted a little when he poured the whiskey; proud of his own brew, no doubt.

Lacy tried a sip, and realized right away that that was no way to do it. He tipped his head back and threw the glass-full down. It hit hard enough.

"That stuff is just poison," the barkeep said. Without teeth, there was nothing much to keep his tongue in his mouth when he talked. "You try mine."

What the hell!

"Okay for one shot," Lacy said, and put two bits down to cover for the first glass.

And damned if the man hadn't been right; his whiskey *was* better than the railroad company's. He'd added cayenne pepper to it. Something like that.

"Good?"

"Not bad," Lacy said. "Not bad at all." He put a dime down for it. This fellow made good dime whiskey.

"Mind if I ask what you put in there in the way of pepper? Is that cayenne?"

The bar-keep was happy to talk about his work. "Hell,

no! *Cayenne*? I wouldn't touch that shit with a ladle! What you taste in there is a double handful jalapany peppers straight up from old Mexico! Double-handful and all mushed up. That's what I use.''

"Fancy that." Lacy put down a second dime for a second shot.

"Look out it don't do yore teeth like it done his'n!" One of the loafers—and not sounding all that hopeless drunk, either. There was no mirror behind the bar; Lacy turned to look at the man. He was a young fellow with a scraggly beard and bright blue eyes, some bloodshot, now. He had a Peacemaker stuck into the side of his waistband. Lacy caught the dim gleam of oil on the steel, and kept that in mind. The man took care of the revolver; it might mean the revolver had also been taking care of the man.

"Hasn't yet," Lacy said to the young man, and raised his glass to him. "Care for a snort?"

The young man shook his head. "I thank you, but I guess I've had enough." He got up off the bench, nodded in a friendly fashion, and ducked his way out through the door. He was tall, about six-foot three or four, Lacy thought. On the bum, too, it had looked like; one of his dirty knees had been poking through a hole in his pants leg. . . Probably had ridden a freight's belly into Clayton, been found and kicked off. It didn't pay to go up against railroad guards; they'd just step back and wire for some railroad detectives to come and blow your head off. *Detectives* was a courtesy call for those fellows; hired back-shooters was more like it. . .though good men had worked for the railroads, Thompson and some others. . .

"Havin' another?" the barkeep said.

"Nope, better not. It'll spoil me for the usual stuff you get on the trail." The barkeep couldn't have been better pleased than to hear that.

"Well, what about some ginch, then?" He winked and leaned in close. "I wouldn't try to fool a grow'd up man about it. The lady is nothin' to write to home concernin', but I swear she's clean as a spring shoat! Washes that thing every single day!"

"It's a temptation," Lacy said, "a dire temptation; but I'd do better to let it pass. My foreman will be expecting my sore butt back to camp, pronto." The barkeep nodded sadly, and Lacy noticed he didn't have to ask what foreman, or what outfit. Clayton might be half-dead, but it wasn't blind.

"Now," Lacy said, "tell me about your beer."

A half-hour later, he had heard all about the barkeep's beer. He made that, too: prime barely-mash, yeast, and hops—double cooked, syruped, rested and cooled. Then fortified, just a mite.

"Draw me a keg," Lacy said.


When he left the Red Rooster, lugging the keg under his arm, Lacy saw the tall young man standing out on the road, waiting for him. Lacy swung the keg under his left arm to free his gun-hand. "Howdy," he said to the man, "still got my teeth, at least so far." The tall man smiled.

"Well, I doan mean to be troublin' yuh," he said —sounded real deep South. "I was wonderin' if thar might be a job with yore outfit?"

"Might be," Lacy said. "You ever work a ranch?"

The young man thought about that for a moment. "No," he said, "I reckon I ain't. Done a lot of farm work, though." Thought of lying, then decided not. Either honest, or no fool. . .

"Have a horse?"

"No, suh."

"I have to haul this keg, so I can't put you up on the horse as well, but why don't you come on out, walking, and have a talk with our foreman. He's a fierce old man, but a fair one. Might be we could use another hand."

The young man nodded, said "much obliged," took the keg while Lacy got mounted, then handed it up to him. He walked along beside the horse, tripping once or twice in the road ruts—it occurred to Lacy that it might have been some time since the man had eaten—and when Lacy mentioned that there was a good chance of trouble coming to the outfit, didn't seem put off by that. A likely-enough man, all in all. Old Meager'd be sure to give the fellow a meal, at least, if he didn't hire him.

Meager, as it turned out, did both. He left the man sitting by the fire—eating cold beef and biscuits like a lobo wolf, while a couple of the men wandered by, looking him over—and came over to the corral where Lacy had just been stacked hard on his head by one of the new horses—a piebald white with a whiter eye.

"What do you think of that horse, Mister Lacy?" the old man said, cocking his stove-pipe hat down so the brim would shade his eyes.

"I think it's a wall-eyed son-of-a-bitch," Lacy said. He'd heard his neck-bone click when he'd landed in the dust, and thought for an instant his neck had been broken. He wasn't young enough—or fit enough—to wrangle horses, and that was the truth.

"You're no wrangler," old Meager said. "Too old." This last said with some satisfaction.

"I know it. You don't have to tell me."

"Well, now, you tell *me* what you think of this Parsons boy you brought in."

"I didn't know his name. I think he'd do. I think he'd be a good hire; looks handy with a gun."

"I'm more concerned is he handy with horses."

"I would say that he is, likely."

The old man heaved a gusty sigh. Lacy caught a whiff of dinner and plug tobacco. "I hope so," Meager said, "because he's hired on."

By dark ("—and make it a light sleep and a short one, boys," the old man had said. "We're moving out fast and early so share that damned bad beer out and don't punish it!") by dark, the tall man, Parsons, was double-fed, beer'd, and dressed up in a catch-all donation of shirts, socks, trousers, smalls, and a hat. But no-one had spare boots, so he was left in his old brogans.

People watched with some interest while he roped out a horse for himself from the new bunch—a stout short-coupled brown—saddled it, and gave it a ride.

The first ride was short. You could see right away he was a farm boy, the way he sat the animal, his legs stuck out in front of him like sticks, and leaning into the brown's mane hard with the other end of him. He was bent on the brown like a safety-pin.

The second ride was short, too, but on the third ride, he stuck. And Lacy noticed that however high the boy bounced, the Peacemaker stayed put in his waistband.

Altogether, a good addition, he thought. Might do to ride drag with Bud. Young eyes, young ears. . . Because the Company was surely going to jump them, going back.

Sure as hell.


For the first two days and nights, there was nothing but riding and work.

Meager sent men out to ride the flanks; Lacy scouted; and Buddy and the new man, Parsons, rode drag. They were getting along fine on the trail, the men working hard—and kept on the alert by the chances of an ambush—and the stock driving well. They'd even had the luck of rain. A storm, likely the one Lacy had seen building, had swept through, and the small gullies in the folds of the prairie had turned to slight runs. The little flows would be dried-up and gone, soon enough, but they were more than handy for the drive. No side trips for springs or sinks.

Old Meager was in great spirits, whether from anticipation of a fight—he'd spent an evening in camp target-shooting with his big Walker Colt, which sounded like artillery letting off, and had hit the tomato cans more often than he'd missed them; better than fair shooting with such a hand cannon—or from the pleasure of bringing a solid herd of good horses out to Angle Iron. The men were always roping and catching-up one of the new horses, claiming them for their strings and having fist-fights over them.

The pleasure of the work, and the good eating One-eye Manuel was cooking up for them, kept all the crew easy and sassy in the grass. And the weather was fine: hot and bright by day, cool and breezy at night. They all lay out at night, under the light of stars as white and dense as spilled flour, and sang songs or told cow-poking stories or ghost stories about peoples' dead children coming back and standing by the back door of their cabins and crying to their mammas for supper.

They'd all lie out there in the green-smelling grass, full of pinto beans and chili-pepper beef, puffing on roll-your-owns, or cob pipes, looing up at the stars and listening to whoever was telling the story. . . Old man Meager told the best ones. He swore that every one of them was true.

Now and again, a night guard would ride in, tilt himself a tin-cup of coffee from the big pot over the firebed, and then roll himself into his blankets. And another man would get up, complaining, and take his piss outside the camp and down-wind, and go to saddle up to take his turn walking his horse around the herd, seeing that the stakes and lines of the night corral were still standing and held taut enough, and to swing out from the herd a bit, rifle across his saddle-bow, to listen for riding sounds, for hoofbeats or bit-jingling, or neighing, that would mean that the Company had sent its people out to call in the night.

It was, all in all, about the sweetest drive of stock that Lacy had ever known. The easiest, and most pleasureful in good company. He'd cut out a horse he named Notch-ear, and rode it to spell Tiger in the afternoons. Notch-ear was a bony black with a long stride. He had some bottom to him, and would scoot some, too, if he was popped on the butt with a rope-end.

Taken all in all, it was a good three days—until the evening.

# CHAPTER TWENTY-TWO

The sun was low, turning red from gold.

They had the bunch spread out in a fair trotting line, the ponies looking as fresh as when they'd started. Fresher; they'd come into shape after the train trip up to Clayton. Old Meager was riding beside the chuck wagon, having words with One-eye Manuel, something fierce about the coffee, when Lacy rode in.

The black, Notch-ear, had picked up a pebble in his left fore three miles out front of the drive, and he'd still limped after Lacy dug it out of his hoof. Lacy'd started walking him back to meet the drive until the limp eased off. No good riding that sore hoof, but soon, walking just got too damn slow. It was the wrong time of day to be afoot.

Lacy patted the black, mounted him, and rode him back to the trailherd at a slow trot. He could get the sorrel saddled and ride out for one more sweep before dark. It was coming on time for trouble.

He rode past the point of the horse-herd; nodded to old Snell and trotted on in. Then he felt the black mis-step; time to get off the animal, hurry or not, or the black would pace shy from here on out. As he swung down from the saddle, Lacy tugged his lariot free and searched through the dust for the sorrel. Out of the corner of his eye, he saw the chuckwagon jouncing toward him. Old Meager riding alongside saying something about boiling coffee.

Right then, Lacy heard the shouting. One man calling. Coming in. He dropped the lariat, reached up and dragged the Sharps out of the boot.

As he got the rifle clear, Lacy saw the new man, Parsons, galloping in. He'd run out from under his hat, and he had his revolver in his hand.

Lacy turned, looking for a God-damned horse that could run. He knew Bud was dead. The boy was certainly dead.

Meager pulled up beside him and swung stiffly out of his saddle.

"Take this one and move out, Mister Lacy!"

Lacy was up on the roan and lining out for Parsons, and he heard the old man calling after him, "I'll get us set for 'em here!"

Parsons turned his horse to meet him, and Lacy reached over the roan's neck to gather a handful of Parsons' shirt.

"*The boy*! Why did you leave that boy?"

Parsons shook his head. "He was down, Mistuh Lacy! He was down and dead! I sweah it!" He looked scared that Lacy would kill him. He still had his pistol in his hand, but he made no try.

"Turn that horse around, you son-of-a-bitch! We're riding back there."

Parsons looked as though he might argue, after all, then he changed his mind. The drive was boiling behind them, old Meager roaring like a lion, the men galloping in, circling the herd to a halt. "Ride out," Lacy said to Parsons. "I'll be right behind you."

In a short run, the noise and shouting were behind them,

and as they reached a flat, Lacy booted Meager's roan up beside Parsons' pony.

He raised his voice over the sounds of the hooves. "How many? How many were there?"

Parsons shook his head as he rode. "I don't know, Mister Lacy! It was a rifle shot hit Buddy—an' I heard horses comin' in."

Lacy thought of killing Parsons right then and there. But it had been his fault, picking the man and bringing him to camp. He'd had the notion that Parsons might be tough, in a quiet way, and that notion had looked to be wrong. Dead wrong for Bud Manugian. This son-of-a-bitch had left him where he'd fallen and run like a rabbit.

Lacy looked to the right and left as they rode, looking for movement on the slight rises, horses riding up from the swales of grass.

Nothing. Nothing but the sound of their hooves, the clouds of grasshoppers buzzing away before them. He hauled back on the reins, and pulled the big roan to a stop: Parsons drew rein to match him, sticking with the sweating brown as it sidled and bucked.

They sat the panting, blowing horses. . .listening.

*Pop. Pop.* Small firecracker sounds behind them.

The Company men were attacking the camp—going for the horses.

Parsons started to rein around, to head back, but Lacy reached out and took his bridle. "We're going on, Parsons; Meager knows what he's about back there."

Parsons shrugged, and then spurred the brown to keep up as Lacy kicked the roan into a gallop.

They found Bud half-a-mile down the trail. Far enough so that they couldn't hear the sounds of the shooting from camp. Far enough so that there was no sound at all when they'd dismounted, except the sounds of their horses—and

Bud's pony, Blackie—munching on the grass. Some birds singing far away, to the south.

Bud lay in the deep grass, on his side, as if he was curling up for sleep. But when Lacy bent to look closer, he saw that one of the boy's eyes was open and staring, as blank as a stone. The other eye was squeezed shut, as if Buddy was winking at him.

Lacy walked around the boy, and saw where the round had gone into him. High in the center of the back. Lacy laid the Sharps down in the grass, took his Barlow knife out of his pocket, knelt, and cut the shirt open over the wound, to take a look at it. He'd seen that bullet's work a hundred times.

Parsons still had his Peacemaker gripped in his hand. Had had, since the trouble started. Probably figured it gave him an edge in case of trouble. Lacy saw the gleam of oil on the fine blued steel. No question the man took care of that piece. His riding was a lot better than it had been. . .

And this was all nobody's fault but Lacy's. His fault alone, for being so careless.

Lacy picked the Sharps up from the grass, cocked it, and shot Parsons through the chest.

At that last instant, Parsons had tried to level the Peacemaker; but he hadn't been ready. Too young for the job. He must have expected some theater-play out of Lacy, if he figured out how Buddy was killed. Some theater-play, and cursing, before the shooting started.

Parsons had been too young for the job. He'd seen Lacy pick the Sharps up, and that was all right. Damn sure the man wasn't going to just leave a rifle in the grass. And then Lacy had cocked the Sharps. Then, Parsons caught on.

A blink too late.

The Sharps was meant for buffalo. The fifty-caliber slug had blasted out in a cloud of fine black-powder smoke, crossed seven feet of Texas air, and struck Parsons like a locomotive. It drove into his chest, and smashed his bones and opened his upper body along its seams. Parsons split like a baked yam, and blood blew out of him in a mist.

Lacy left the two horses, and Parsons. . . and Bud, and rode the roan for the camp, the warm-barreled Sharps across his saddlebow. He hoped with all his heart that there would be a chance to kill some more of the Company men. He hoped it with all his heart.

But he knew whose fault the boy's death was. A ragged drifter with a plausible tale. A poor farm-boy with a fine Peacemaker Colt. The Company had sent him there to sign on, if he could. To do what scouting and back-shooting he could. He'd known the time they'd come raiding, and he'd shot Buddy in the back to let them go riding by. It had been no rifle bullet that had gone into Buddy's back. It had been a .45.

A tall, raggedy, Deep-South farm boy. And Lacy had ushered him into the game.

Lacy ran the laboring roan hard down the flats, then eased him up the rise—and sat the saddle, looking out over the camp to see how the land lay.

It lay well enough.

Meager had gathered five or six men on foot beside the chuckwagon, using their rifles to keep the raiders from stampeding the horse-herd. The two-strand rope corral was still holding, though Lacy could see the horses milling in fear at the dust and yells and gunshots. A few animals had jumped the line and were running free, but most of the herd was held.

Meager had left the other two or three men mounted, to ride in and out of the fight, keep the raiders worried about their backs.

And it had worked fine, up to now. (Lacy could hear the old man bellowing like a bull down there in all that racket.) But time was running against them.

There had to be twelve, maybe fifteen of the raiders. Oklahoma men, by the look of their hats—sent south. Probably been promised the horses. And they were harder cases than the cowboys.

Three men lay in the dirt around the chuckwagon. And Lacy saw Wry Neck Tom Clark down and dead beside his paint just on this side of the fire-pit.

Too many down, already.

Lacy swung out of the saddle, and knelt at in the high grass of the ridgeline. He was only twenty. . .thirty feet higher than the camp, but it was enough.

About four-hundred yards. A long shot.

He cocked the Sharps, leveled it—bracing his elbow against his raised knee—and drew a fine bead on a man on a small dun horse. The fellow was wearing a vest and a plug hat; he looked to be shouting orders to some riders near him.

Lacy shot him out of his saddle. And, some surprised at the hit at this distance, shifted his stance to the side of the drift of powdersmoke to fire again.

They'd spotted him, now, and as he knelt in the grass, smelling the mingled scent of flowers and gunsmoke, Lacy heard the twang of rifle slugs humming past him.

Long range for carbines. He heard the raiders shouting around the camp, the quickening crack of shots as Meager poured it on.

But there were too damn many. Lacy took a sight on a rifleman who was sitting his horse down there as calm as could be, levering and firing up at Lacy as if he had all evening to make his shot.

Lacy shot at him—and missed.

And paid for the miss with a stinging bullet crease along his upper arm. He rolled to the side without thinking when he felt the impact, glanced down and saw it was nothing much, reloaded, and raised the Sharps for another shot.

Too late to try for that rifleman again. He was gone somewhere in the clouds of dust, the crash of gun fire around the camp.

No time, anyway. Three horsemen were lining out up the rise toward him. Coming fast, and shooting.

They were good. He felt the brim of his Stetson ticked by a round that knocked it sideways on his head, and heard the scream of his horse going down as bullets found it. His fault, should have left the animal further down the slope.

He blew the head off the first rider.

For an instant it was as though the man's head had turned to a wet red flag whipping, spraying out behind him as he rode. Then he was gone.

No time left. Lacy dove to the side again, rolling, trying to reload the damn Sharps while the two rode down at him shooting. . . shooting.

He came up to his knees, saw a bearded man with his mouth open. And shot that son-of-a-bitch through the shoulder. Spun him out of his saddle into the air like an acrobat.

Lacy jumped back as the third horseman fired down at him. The round went down somewhere; Lacy felt it thump into the ground deep between his feet. Up went that man's revolver to be cocked. A Remington .44. Everything moving so slowly. . .

Lacy drew and shot the man twice. Once under his raised arm. Once right into his ribs, to drill him side to side.

Then he stood up with everything going as fast as it usually did, and the horses milling and kicking around him, and the two men flopping and one gasping for breath. A terrible smell of gunpowder. Enough to make a man sick.

Lacy didn't move from where he stood. He felt like staying still. Just moving his wrist, taking careful aim, he shot each of the downed men again. They were moving, lying half-buried in the deep green grass, so he had to judge where their chests and backbones were as he shot them.

Even so, he got it done with just one round each.

Then he felt like moving, and walked through the grass on down the ridge, reloading the Bisley Colt, and looking for some more men to shoot.

There was no one near him for a moment or two, and Lacy heard the steady, regular fire from the chuckwagon. Now, with things seeming not so noisy, he could even make out the slow, regular boom of old Meager's Walker revolver.

Then he saw a horseman riding by. As often happens in fights, the man was riding right past him without stopping or firing at him. In fights, a man could lose his nerve in one minute, and find it in another. Or a man could just not feel like shooting at someone right then. Could feel like not making that much extra noise.

The man seemed to be a small fellow. He had a plug hat on, and Lacy could see the red sleeves of his long-underwear showing below his shirt-sleeves.

Lacy extended his arm and took a careful aim, then he fired at the man's back.

He'd aimed high, to hit him between the shoulder-blades, but hit him in the small of the back instead. The small man threw up his arms and fell sideways off his horse. His foot caught in the stirrup, but the horse slowed and stopped, and didn't drag him.

By the time Lacy had walked over there, the man's foot

was free, and he was up on his elbow in the grass, feeling at his holster for his revolver. But he had dropped it when he fell.

"You son of a bitch!" the man yelled at Lacy. "Did you shoot me?"

Lacy nodded.

"In the back," the man said. He looked white as milk with the shock of being hurt so badly. "You shot me in the back, you yellow dog."

"Not with this one," Lacy said, and he shot the small man in the heart.

Even so, it took the fellow a minute to die. He fell back and moaned and gripped at his chest with his hands. He gripped and pulled at himself there as if he could pull the bullet back out and make everything all right again.

Now, it was very quiet.

Lacy heard horses running, and looked up and saw the Oklahomans riding off, riding north away from the camp. Four of them riding, one going double with an injured man.

The rest were down, and hurt bad or dead. He heard a man shouting by the chuckwagon. Except for that shouting, everything was quiet.

Lacy felt fairly well. Not sick to his stomach. Maybe a little tired. . .

# CHAPTER TWENTY-THREE

Lacy rode alone through high grass in the morning. Just a few miles out from Angle Iron, now.

Old Meager had stayed behind to clean up the camp, bandage the wounded, and bury the dead. The old man had the notion that the Company might have sent a couple of riders out to the Iron to do what damage they could, maybe throw a scare into Miss Louise while they were at it. Easy enough for the raiders to do last evening, if they'd had a mind to spare some riders for it.

But that didn't seem like Central Cattle Company style to Lacy. That outfit liked a sidling, sideways gait—at least when it came to owners and ladies—to people who mattered more than common cowpokers did. Lacy doubted that the Company wanted to get into a shooting with a lady. It would be a sure way to get the Rangers up from Austin at the double.

Still, he'd been glad enough to ride on ahead. He didn't need to see Bud Manugian buried to know he was dead. He needed no reminder about that—or about who it was who'd picked up Parsons to ride with them.

The Oklahomans had lost—and lost hard. The Company wouldn't be pleased about that. Wouldn't be pleased with whoever had arranged it, either.

Four Iron hands were dead: Tom Clark, Charlie Jorgensson, Bud, and another man. And three more had been shot, and hurt badly enough to have to wagonride when Meager brought them in. Even so, the raiders had been hurt worse. Six dead, and four down and wounded. Another man might have put a bullet through the heads of the men that were hurt. Not old Meager. He'd bring them in with his own, heal them up, then take them down to the cottonwoods and hang them decently.

Lacy was riding one of the new-bought horses, a long-backed pinto without a name. The pinto had a rough jog, but he was a stayer.

Lacy made the ranch before noon.

He pulled up on a slight rise just back of the remuda corrals, and looked Angle Iron over. There was no mess, no trouble to be seen. Two hands, Phil Walker and another man of the left-behinds, were nailing shingles on the horse-born roof, and making a damn slow job of it, too. Slacking-off without old Meager around.

Lacy didn't see Miss Louise outside, but there was smoke drifting up from the chimney of the house.

No trouble. The Company had been content to try for the horse herd.

Lacy reined the pinto down the gentle slope to the north corral. There was a fair-filled stock tank beside the fence. He pulled up, swung out of the saddle, tied the pinto to a rail, and stripped off his clothes. They stank of gun-powder and travel sweat, horse-lather and spoiled, dried blood. Lacy saw one of the men on the barn roof looking over at him, and he gave the man a wave, picked up a clump of thick grama grass, and stepped buck naked into the big water trough to wash.

He heard the man call him from the barn roof, but paid him no mind. He rolled in the muddy water like an otter, and stood up soaked and dripping to scrub himself with the handful of bunch-grass.

"Say, now, Lacy—did they make any try for the horses?" Walker was standing by the corral fence.

"They made a good try."

"Oh, dammit—god-dammit to hell! They get 'em?"

"They did not." Lacy sat back down in the water, and bent forward to duck his head, raised it and ran the water out of his hair with his hands.

"They killed some of our people, trying?" Tom Clark had been a particular friend of Walker's.

"They killed Tom," Lacy said to him. "And some others, too." He climbed out of the trough. "I'm sorry, Walker. Tom put up a damn good fight." Still naked, he pulled the saddle and bridle from the pinto, and rump-slapped the animal into the corral. Then he picked up his dirty clothes and his gun-belt, and walked across the yard to the bunkhouse.

Walker asked him no more questions, and didn't follow him. At the bunkhouse door, Lacy looked back and saw Walker standing against the corral fence crying into his bandanna. Tom Clark and Walker had been raised together in Oregon. Walker had been an orphan, Lacy'd heard, and Clark's family had taken him in and raised the boys together.

Lacy dug clean clothes out of his war-bag; old Snell had brought the whole kit and kaboodle out from Miss Maynard's for him in the supply wagon. All his things had been fresh washed and folded, and there'd been a written message folded in there for him from Silky Perkins.

He finished dressing, wiped some trail-dirt from his

boots, and walked across the yard to the house to see Miss Louise and tell her what had happened. As he walked, he heard the hammers rapping on the horse-barn roof.

The day was sunny, and very still, except for that sound.

Miss Louise took him into her parlor, and went to her kitchen to make him a cup of coffee. Then she came and sat down, and he told her.

She hadn't asked him anything at all when he'd first come in the door, and had acted calm as a woman at a Sunday school lunch. But when she came back in with the coffee, Lacy saw that her hands were shaking.

"The men. . ." she said.

Most ranchers would have asked about the horses.

"Four hands dead," Lacy said. "And some wounded."

She dropped her cup of coffee on the carpet, and sat in the chair and let the coffee lie, soaking the dark pattern at her feet. She put her hand over her mouth.

"Bud was the worst," Lacy said. "Killed through my carelessness." He knelt down to pick up her coffee cup from the carpet. "The other three died fighting." He reached up to put the cup on a small table, and Miss Louise leaned forward and fell into his arms like a shot bird.

Lacy had a time to keep both of them from rolling on the floor; Miss Louise was a big lady. She didn't say a word, but clung to Lacy and buried her head in his shoulder, and wept like a child. He felt the damp of her tears on his shirt. She was sobbing as if it were years of weeping she was getting done. She couldn't seem to stop it.

He got her half up on her feet, and forced her away from him a little. Plain enough before, Miss Louise was a sad sight to see weeping, her bony horseface wrinkled-up and red, running with tears. Ugly as could be. . .

"I'm sorry," Lacy said. And he didn't know if it was for getting Buddy killed by that Reb back-shooter—or just all the hurt that he and men like him brought to women out here. *Sorry* was what he felt, and "sorry" was what he said. . . for everything that made her cry.

"Forgive me," she said. "I'm dreadfully— Forgive me." And she abruptly straightened up, and stood with her hand on the back of a chair. With her other hand, she took a handkerchief from the pocket of her dress and started to dry her eyes. "What about the horses?" she said, looked around her as if she didn't know the room—and fainted dead away.

It was the damndest thing.

Lacy hadn't had a woman faint since Cora Ripley had passed out on the grand staircase of the San Francisco opera-house—and that had been from lacing too tight to show Phoebe Snow what was what.

That was considerably different from having a big horse of a ranch-woman stretched out on her Turkey carpet at his feet.

Lacy knelt down, got his arms under her, and managed to stand with her in his arms. She was a heavy woman. He carried her through to the bedroom door, got a hand free to twist the knob, carried her in, and laid her out on the bed.

Why the hell she didn't have a woman here to take care of her, not even some Mexican maid-servant.

Miss Louise was lying stretched out on a bright red and yellow comforter, looking sallow and lank as a corpse in her dark brown dress. Lacy was looking for the wash-stand, to get her a glass of water, when she sighed and her eyes opened.

She stared at him for a moment, then her eyes widened

and she sat straight up on the bed, blushing red as fire.

"Mister Lacy, I've been very silly, I'm afraid. I never, *never*. . . I never *have* swooned away like some spoiled girl. . ." She swung her feet to the floor, and tried to stand up.

"Why don't you just rest, ma'am. . ."

She sat back down on the bed. "Did you tell me about the horses?" she said, and she looked across the room. "I wonder if you would pour me a glass of water, please."

Lacy found a glass on the wash-stand, filled it from the pitcher, and brought it over to her. "The horses are in good shape. I don't think we lost any of them. Mister Meager will be bringing them in early tomorrow."

She drank the water, and sat on the edge of the bed with her head bent. "That's very good," she said. "I believe that because of you and Mister Meager. . . I believe that we will be able to. . . keep the Iron. . . to all stay together here."

"Yes, ma'am, I should think so. If you get some good young riders, now—" He was sorry he'd said that, because the woman put her face in her hands and began to cry again.

"Now, listen," Lacy said, and he took her by the shoulders. "All this crying and fainting and all that is just a waste of time!" He shook her a little. "What did you imagine *would* happen, ranching out here? Some thieves tried to take your place. You could give it up—or fight. That's all there is to it!"

She nodded and said yes, that was right, her voice still muffled in her hands. Lacy went to her dresser, opened the top drawer, and took out a clean, folded handkerchief. She had a stack of them in there, like most women. He came back to the bed and put the handkerchief into her hand, and she raised her face and began mopping at it, drying her tears.

She looked so plain, so sad, that Lacy said: "Oh, come on, now, come on, now," and bent and kissed her on the cheek. After he did that, she said something, and then turned her mouth up to him like an ugly, newborn filly, hungry and desperate for feeding. She kissed him with little ignorant pecks, as if she'd never kissed a man at all.

He sat beside the bed and hugged her, wondering how the hell to get out of this, and she hugged him back. "I'm so alone," she said. "I'm so alone."

He held her off from him a little, trying to think of something to say to her, but she gripped at him, clutching at his shoulders. "What shall I do?" she said. "What shall I *do*?" and her face was wild.

Lacy couldn't think of anything special to say to her, so he said: "There, now," and kissed her like a lover.

She sighed and relaxed against him for a moment, but her mouth was hard against his lips. "Take it easy, now, dear," he said. "Open your lips, and be nice and soft for me."

She made a sound, and slowly he felt her lips soften against his. He kissed at her gently until her mouth began to open, and he felt her body easing in his arms.

"There, now."

He leaned back with her onto the bed, kissing her, and felt her mouth open wide under his, the wet and breath from her, and he slid his tongue into her and felt her twist against him for a moment, as if she were frightened. But he held her still, and felt, after a while, the slow, moist stirring of her tongue against his. She didn't know what to do, and Lacy found with some surprise that that excited him. He coaxed her, tickled her, slowly drew her tongue out with his, and licked and gently sucked at it.

She groaned something, after a while, and tried to move away, to turn her head away to catch her breath; but he didn't let her go. His cock was up hard, hurting in the tightness of his trousers. He bore down on her, working his mouth on hers, thrusting his tongue into her as if he were fucking her.

He felt her stiffen as she seemed to realize the rhythm, what the rhythm meant, and tried to pull away again, saying something muffled against his mouth.

But he didn't let her go.

When she finally relaxed against him, moaning into his mouth, Lacy held her close for a moment, then pulled away from her and sat up.

"Get up and take your clothes off, Louise."

She lay still on the bright comforter, her eyes tight shut, and shook her head. "No," she said. "I can't do that."

He got off the bed, reached down and gripped her arm, and lifted her up. "Get up and get undressed. Do it right now."

Lacy stood by the side of the bed and began taking his clothes off. What had started as comforting, was something else, now. He was tired and still angry from the fighting; and he had a hard cock, and a shy, big, bony woman to put it in. He stripped his vest and shirt off and threw them onto a chair.

Louise Bristol sat on the edge of the bed and watched him.

He hauled his boots off, then unbuttoned his trousers and skinned out of them, and his longjohns.

She stared at his cock.

Lacy walked over in front of her. "Is this the first one you've seen?" She stared at it, blushing, looking more like a horse than ever, her brown eyes wide, her long brown hair coming down in tangles from the wrestling they'd done on her bed.

Lacy reached down, picked up one of her limp hands, and put it on him. She gripped at his swollen cock almost

214

absently, staring at it. Then she looked up at him. "Please help me, Mister Lacy," she said.

"I'll help you," Lacy said.

He bent and took her by the shoulders, and pushed her back down on the bed. Then he reached down, gathered the material of her skirts in his hands and threw them up, over her thighs. "No," she said, and she tried to hit at him with her hands. He caught both her wrists in one of his hands, gripped them hard, and forced her arms up over her head. Then, naked, he straddled her, pinning her down.

With his free hand, he reached down and caught one of her knees and pulled it up hard and to the side, spreading her out. He saw the frill of her petticoats and under-drawers, and held her legs wide with his while he felt into her with his free hand.

"Oh, no! Oh, my God!" She struggled against him, writhing and kicking, straining her head up to try to bite his forearm where he held her wrists.

His hand slid through the soft folds of cotton; he felt the long, strong muscles of her thighs as she tried to kick out at him. She had long, solid legs. Handsome legs, under all that skirting. Legs like a Flora-dora girl, a dancer, long, and heavy-curved, and muscled.

She was gasping from the effort of struggling against him, saying please don't. . . please don't do this. . . And she arched her back, rearing up off the bed as he felt the fat, soft, warm mound hidden under the pleats and cambric. "Oh, please don't!" Her voice was rising into a scream, and he let her wrists go and put his hand over her mouth.

She began to strike at him with her fists, but he paid no attention to that. He drove his hand harder up between her legs, felt the mound full in his palm, and squeezed it hard. She gasped and cried out something into his smothering hand, tried to turn her head to get free of it, to get a breath.

Lacy leaned on her hard. And began to worry the cloth away from her cunt, pulling it aside with his fingers, tearing a strip of cotton that was in his way. He tore the piece of cloth in half, and felt the touch of curly hair against his fingers. He wormed his hand in and felt the whole thing, hot and hairy, swollen against his grip.

She heaved underneath him, writhing and twisting to be free, but he held her, smothering her mouth, and squeezed and probed at her cunt, tickling with his finger for the moisture, the wet at her hole. He found it under her fur—a narrow, hot, oily place, folded deep. He tickled it, stroked it, reached in another finger so that he could get into it, spread it a little. He felt the stickiness as the lips parted, just a little in there. And he found the narrow, small, wetness, and slid a finger deep into her.

She shouted against his hand, and hit at his face with her fists, her long, strong legs thrashing, trying to get him out of her—away from her. As she kicked, Lacy felt the wet hole moving, squeezing against his finger. He felt the touch of her cherry against his finger-tip. His finger was swimming in hot oil.

He took his hand from her mouth, and as she whooped and gasped for breath, he came down onto her and kissed her deep, breathing his breath out into her, letting her gasp in his breath, his spittle, his tongue. And he took his finger out of her cunt, gripped his cock in his hand, fumbled—and put it to her.

He felt the rough touch of her hair against the tip of his cock, then the small slippery heat. And he got it into her. She struggled against him, and tried to bite his lips as he kissed her.

He grunted, set himself—and drove his swollen cock.

She yelped in pain and arched her back to throw him off—and as she did, he slid all the way into her and broke her maidenhead.

216

Lacy held himself still, then, and felt her cunt gripping, squeezing at him. Miss Louise lay still under him, now, panting, trembling against him.

He pulled half out of her, and she groaned. Then he gently thrust into her again, going easy. Sliding a little out of her, then in again. Rocking gently above her, feeling the slippery folds of her, inside. There was no sound but their breathing, and the soft, wet noises he made thrusting into her. Lacy bent his head to kiss her gently, kissing her lips, the softness of her throat under the long jaw. She lay beneath him, still, her eyes squeezed shut like a child's. He moved on her, and now he could smell the blood where he had torn her open, the fish-glue smell of her cunt.

He began to move harder, driving into her harder, smacking into her. She began to grunt with the impacts. He felt her long legs shifting against him as she accommodated herself, tried to avoid the pain as he shoved it slowly into her.

"Please," she said. Her eyes were open now; she was staring up at him. He bent to kiss her again. He whispered to her, "My handsome. . . handsome little mare." He felt that he loved her, a little, and he whispered to her, and hugged her, and kissed her like a lover.

She moaned into his mouth, and he sucked gently at her tongue, and felt her begin to move under him, straining, and raising herself to let him go deeper in. She began, slowly, to work with him. He felt her raising her knees, spreading them wider to let him in against her, to let him get deeper into her.

He thrust harder. He felt the jizzum rising in him, hurting the small of his back with the pleasure. The wet rawness of her cunt was holding him, gripping at him as he pulled out of her—then drove in all the way.

"Oh, my God!" she said. "Oh, dear God, I love it!"

Her long legs strained up, up on either side of him, the

smell of her cunt was strong fish; her hair there was sopping wet with blood and juice. He began to fuck her faster, digging into her, driving into her as if to injure her—to kill her.

She screamed, heaved her hips up against him, and reached down to grip his buttocks, to hold him still against her. Her cunt grew fat and hotter, clutching him in, and she shook against him.

And the pleasure of her coming off made his pleasure greater.

She was already easing, murmuring in his arms, when Lacy groaned and gave it to her. Pumped and pumped and gave it all to her. Gave her everything.


An hour later, they were still in bed together, joking each other, and playing a poor game of checkers on the tumbled bedclothes. They'd lost half the pieces in the linen, and had to rely on each other's word for the crowned kings lost. Lying and tickling had proved the best way of the game.

It was the second game, and the best they'd played, and Lacy was just claiming victory when they heard someone calling from the yard.

Calling, and knocking on the door.

# CHAPTER TWENTY-FOUR

It was Talbot.

The big red-faced lawyer stood sweating on the ranch-house porch, his fine gray suit sweat wet under the arms. It was a hot afternoon, but not that hot.

Lacy had taken his time dressing, and coming to answer the door. Louise was still fluttering around the bedroom, in a panic that it might be old Mister Meager, ridden in early and knocking at her door. She feared what the old man would think of her if he knew.

"What do you want out here, Talbot? —Miss Louise is in her room; she isn't feeling well."

"Well, now, well, now, that's a shame," the lawyer said. "I'm certainly sorry to hear it."

"Are you now, you son of a bitch?" Lacy reached out and slapped the lawyer across his flushed face. It was a hard blow, and left the pale mark of Lacy's fingers on Talbot's face. The big man turned pale as milk-cheese and stepped back to the porch rail. He didn't offer to hit Lacy back, or even raise his fists. "If this wasn't a lady's house, I'd break your jaw for you, you yellow dog." Lacy was getting angrier and angrier, just looking at the man.

Talbot sat down on the porch rail, and put his hand up to his face, where Lacy'd hit him. He didn't look Lacy in the eye; he looked down at the porch flooring. Lacy could smell the whiskey hazing off the man in the afternoon heat.

"I. . . I was hired by the Fort Worth people, to. . . to be their agent in this area." He glanced up at Lacy, then looked away. His blue eyes were suffused with red. "I had no notion there was to be all this killing."

"If you say one more excusing word to me," Lacy said, "I will take you out in the grass and put a bullet into your head." He turned to go back into the house.

"No, no. . .now, listen to me! I. . .I need your help."

"*My* help?"

"There's a man," the lawyer said. "He came to Bristolton three days ago. He's at the Grand Hotel right now . . ."

"What's that to me?"

Talbot sat on the porch railing and stared off over the corrals. "He's going to kill me," he said to Lacy, still staring out over the yard. "He's going to kill me. . .to silence me about the Central's doings in the north."

"Shit; they're killing you for failing the job."

Talbot had nothing to say.

"Let them kill you, and welcome," Lacy said, and turned and went into the house.

"No—no!" Talbot said, and the big man lunged to his feet and tried to follow Lacy into the house. "You don't understand me!"

"I understand you very well, Mister Talbot," Miss Louise said. She stood at the door to the parlor, as correct a lady as could be, hair up, dress down, neat as a pin. "Get out of my house and get off of my land, or I'll have my men whip you off of it!"

"It's not only me," Talbot said, looking as though he might burst into tears. "This man means to finish their work for them!" He clung to the doorway as if to hold himself up. "They sent him up here in case the. . . in case other things went wrong. I'm telling you he intends to see that Central purchases this property!"

"Why this property, Talbot?" Lacy said. "There are other ranches."

"Not on the right-of-way route for the Texas and Southern, there aren't! The railroad's coming through here, man! It'll be billed-in at the legislature in Austin next year. . ."

"Oh, my God," Miss Louise said.

And he was telling the truth: Lacy knew it. It explained the money and men the Central Cattle Company had put into the fight. A railroad running through the property meant easy shipping for stock and supplies. . . It meant doubling the value of the ranch. More than doubling it.

"Do you see it?" Talbot looked desperate. "This man will murder me! And he'll go for you, as well, Lacy!" He said it with satisfaction. "He'll certainly kill you unless you kill him first!"

"And that's what you want, is it? For me to pull your irons out of the fire? Forget it, Talbot. I'm riding, and I don't give a damn if this fellow cuts your guts out! I apologize for my language, Louise."

"Go on, then, and run!" Talbot said, his face as red as a beet. "No reason you should care for me." His eyes narrowed. "Unless it's money that you want. You seemed to be hungry enough for money, back in town."

"You'd better be going, Talbot," Lacy said. "While you still can."

"I'll give you my horse," Talbot said, "I'll give you the thoroughbred. And stock! I have railroad stock—"

He backed away from the door, still talking, pleading, as Lacy walked toward him.

"Peach will kill the old man. That's what he plans to do!"

"Meager. . .?"

Talbot stopped, halfway down the porch steps. "Yes, the old man. Peach intends to call him out. He knows the old man will fight. Peach will kill him!"

Lacy thought about it; it was exactly what they would do, of course. Once the old man was dead, Louise would be alone. . .alone except for a bunch of cowpokers with no leader or hardcase among them. It would be Central's last try. And it would do the trick for them, too.

"They wouldn't dare to do that," Louise said, coming to the door. "You're a dirty liar, Mister Talbot!"

"Who is this man, Peach?" Lacy said.

Talbot put his hat on to shade himself from the sun on the porch steps. "He's from Chicago, I understand. A murderer named George Peach. I've seen him. He spoke to me once, remarking on the weather, the son-of-a-bitch!" He glanced apologetically at Miss Louise. "But my cousin sent me a note about him. . ."

"What sort of man is he?"

"Will you go and fight him, Lacy? I'll give you anything you ask for."

"What sort of man is he?"

Talbot cleared his throat. "Decent enough to talk to," he said, "if you didn't know what the man was. He looks a dude, a city man. He's young."

"Don't fight him," Miss Louise said to Lacy. "I'm sure there's no need for you to fight him." She looked very frightened. "You are a liar!" she screamed at Talbot. Suddenly, she ran across the porch with her fist raised, to hit at him, and Talbot, trying to say something to her, turned and ran away from her down the porch steps. It was his day for running.

Lacy caught Miss Louise by the arms and held her. "You stay here," he called to Talbot. "You wait." Then he took Miss Louise into the house.

Talbot was standing beside his handsome horse when Lacy came out of the house. Talbot shifted nervously as Lacy walked across the yard to him. The lawyer's nerve was gone; he looked like a huge, frightened baby in a sweaty suit.

"Are you going to do it? Will you fight him?" he said.

"Stand away from my horse," Lacy said. And he went to the big gray's side, and stood for a moment, stroking the marble-smooth hide, running his hand gently over the gray's velvet muzzle. Then, he swung himself up into the saddle; it was a Mexican saddle, and shallower than he liked, but the horse—*Rain*—felt strong as a oak under him.

"Now, listen to me, Talbot," he said. "You leave a bill of sale for this horse with Miss Louise, then you take what plug she'll sell you, and you ride to town and get your goods. One way or another, either this fellow Peach—or I—will kill you if you're still in town tomorrow."

"Yes, I'll go. I'll go," Talbot said. But Lacy had already turned the big gray away, and spurred him into a trot.

He had the gray.

The hire of his gun, after all. No matter that Talbot was more a dog than a man. No matter, either, that Lacy couldn't have ridden off to Mexico and left a brave old man with one arm to be shot down in the street.

He had hired out his gun. . . hired out to kill a man he'd never met. *Hired-out for a horse*.

A scarface drifter with gray in his hair, hired for a killing by the price of a horse. A killing that had to be done, for sure, and would have been tried, thoroughbred or no. But he'd taken the horse, just the same. That was his price.

It made him less than he'd been.

Less than he'd been. . .

Lacy rode easy toward the town. No need to hurry. He'd go to the Grand Hotel, and take a look at the man, tonight. Or search him down to some saloon or crib, see how he stood, how he looked at people, how he carried his gun.

Shoulder holster maybe, if he was a dude. Some thought that sort of rig very slow. And it could be. But John Wesley Hardin used shoulder holsters. Jesse James had, too, for that matter.

The gray was worth it. Lacy felt the ease of the animal under him, its motion, the light and prancing stride. He touched it with the spurs, and the gray responded on the instant, and shifted into a canter, then a lope—all smooth and easy as a rocking chair. A coward, Talbot certainly was, but he'd schooled a fine horse.

Lacy touched the gray into a gallop, and the big horse gathered itself, and strode out, and flew.

When he pulled up, after half a mile, Lacy swung down out of the saddle, and stood waist-high in the buffalo grass. He reached Talbot's canteen down from the saddlebow, uncorked and smelled it to be sure it wasn't filled with whiskey, poured some into the crown of his Stetson and held it to the big horse's muzzle. The great head dipped to it, and drank, the huge dark honey-colored eyes looking down at Lacy as soft and innocent as an angel's.


Lacy rode into town at dark, and went straight to Miss Maynard's, tired, and feeling bad.

The old lady seemed glad enough to see him, and invited him straight into her parlor. Big William was well, and guarding her door.

They talked a while, about business, and the ambush for the horse herd (the people in town had heard wild stories about that fight). And Lacy told Miss Maynard he would be leaving the state. The old lady sighed when she heard that, and rocked a little slower, her bird-hands busy with her tatting.

"Well, you shall have to tell Silky," she said. "I don't hold with a man just riding off without doing the proper."

Lacy said that he would speak to Silky, and he and the old lady sat in companionable silence for a while; he said nothing about George Peach. Every now and then, one of the girls would come to the door to peek at him.

Later, Silky came to get him. Sarah had told her he was in the house, and she'd rushed a customer named Dawes to come to the parlor and take Lacy up to her room.

They went up there, and had dinner, which Sarah brought up and said was a farewell present from Miss Maynard.

When she heard that, Silky gave Lacy a hard look. "Are you going away from me?" she said, and she put her forkful of potato down without tasting it.

"Yes, I am," he said. And she didn't say anything more about it, but went on and finished her potatoes.

She seemed happy enough to get him into bed after dinner. Lacy had been afraid she would smell Louise on him, but she didn't appear to. Too much of a cloud of her own perfume for that, he supposed, and Lacy had feared hurting her feelings by not being up for her. But she didn't seem to notice his being slow; she didn't appear to care about it. The loving seemed as good for her as it had ever been. And afterward, they lay together talking about Mexico, and how he'd write to her from there—and send her something pretty if he had the chance.

"Not a fancy," she said. "Nothin' for a lot money. Just a little pretty is all." And Lacy said he would. He felt he was well-enough out of it, that she hadn't noticed about Louise. He didn't want Silky hurt that way.

At ten o'clock in the evening, with guests already singing in the parlor and tramping up and down the stairs, Lacy turned in bed, and kissed Silky's breast and said goodbye to her. She gave him a kiss, and said goodbye—and slapped him a farewell on the butt as he got out of bed to dress.

"Be careful," she said. "Be careful."

Lacy supposed she meant, in general. "I will," he said. "And I won't forget your pretty."

Silky yawned and sighed, and turned over to go to sleep while he dressed.

When he was dressed, his gun-belt on, he stopped and bent to kiss her on his way to the door. He kissed the soft nape of her neck.

When the door was closed behind him and he was gone, Silky said to the dark, "You smelled of fish, you son-of-a-bitch." Then she cried a long while, said "God-damn all men," and then went to sleep.

# CHAPTER TWENTY-FIVE

Lacy walked down South Street, yawning.

He felt tired-out and stiff as wood. Old and frail, like a dog without a tail. His mother used to say that sometimes. It hadn't made much sense, but it felt right, now. He stretched his arms out, almost knocking a cowpoker's hat off, and rolled his shoulders, trying to ease the muscles of his back. The boardwalk was crowded tonight, men from the stockyards east of town, mostly. Irishmen, they looked like, with their long dish-faces, and pipes and ragged clothes. Considerable of them were drunk, but behaving themselves well enough, tramping along from crib to crib in the flaring lamp light, talking in their odd way, and singing high-pitched as girls. Decent people, probably, and treated like dogs more often than not—but when it came to laborers, Lacy liked the Chinese better. They had more of a sense of humor.

It had been hard to get up out of Silky's bed to come out walking around the town looking for George Peach. It was possible that he was a little scared of finding the man. Wouldn't be the first time he'd been a little scared. A man who wasn't worried about the George Peaches wasn't right. Worried about killing the fellow, too, as he would most assuredly have to try to do. The preachers said that killing a man was like killing a bit of yourself.

They didn't know the half of it. What they said was partly true. But what they didn't know was the pleasure of killing, and the shame at the pleasure. There was no way to know that. To know that killing a man—seeing his lights go out—could be a greater pleasure than any other.

It was the pleasure that rotted gun-men out.

That had spoiled him? It was fair to say it. That had spoiled him.

Could ride away, of course. Could ride, and let Peach at them. Be a nasty surprise for Talbot, to find that Lacy hadn't even tried, but had plain skedaddled with the gray, and not a shot fired. But it would be a nasty surprise for old man Meager. To have some dandy punk from Chicago throw a glass of beer on him in the barroom of the Grand, call him a coward, and ask him to step out into the street.

For if that ever happened, the old man would rise up roaring, hit the street, and reach for that huge Walker Colt without a second thought about it. He'd reach—slow as Michigan molasses—and the Chicago man would shoot him down.

A fair-enough end for an old Texican, perhaps. But it would leave Miss Louise all alone on the Angle Iron. The Company would have that ranch in a month.

It was another fight a famous gunman couldn't run from. The so-famous Buckskin Frank Leslie (Mister Lacy, now) was being called upon to do what he did best.

And how could he have avoided it? Could he have let the Bothwells kill Bud at the fence? Let Abe beat the tar out of him? Let the Bothwells kill Bud in the Two-bit? Though, God knows, he'd only saved the Armenian boy to lose him

228

later. Stayed off the horse-drive, then? Maybe. Maybe he could have stayed off the horse-drive; the boy might be alive if he had. And then stayed out of Miss Louise's bed.

He'd taken advantage of her hurt and loneliness like any Kansas City cadet. God knows it had been his working skill in the old days. And what a sweet piece she'd proved to be. Hard to regret those long, strong legs around him. Hard to regret the first strike into that close cunt.

It was strange for a man to notice his own sliding down. Slower with the Colt, these days, for sure. And with this bullet-cut face. . . And taking a horse for pay to shoot a man. Sliding down-hill, and no mistake about it. The bad, soft spot that'd let him run as a gun-fighter when he was young, had only gotten bigger with the years. Lacy thought that he might never have grown out of being a hard case kid. A spoiled, old-looking kid, now. Nothing much without the gun.

Getting worse all round? Maybe getting worse, all round. A useful tool for some decent people, every once in a while. At best.


At the corner of Second Street and South, he turned and walked up toward Main. Some rough boys were running down Second Street in the dark. They were chasing a dog with tin cans tied to its legs. The dog was making good speed, but a hell of a racket as it ran. The kids were after it, fast as deer; some other torturing idea in mind, probably.

It occured to Lacy that he wouldn't have the patience to wait until tomorrow to call this George Peach out. The damn fellow had no business coming all the way to Texas for trouble. It had been foolish of him.

Might as well find him tonight, and let him know it.

Possible the man was fast, of course. In fact, he was

bound to be fast, or quick, at any rate. And he was likely to be a prime pistol-shot. City toughs were often target shooters. Lacy wondered if he should try for the man out in the dark. City people didn't care for the dark; they liked lighted, cheery places. Darkness might spoil the man's shooting.

Slid down-hill, for sure, angling to get a man at a disadvantage. Had been a time it wouldn't have occurred to try to catch a man off-base. Would have been no reason or need for it.

Lacy walked up Second Street amid the colors of the lamps: blue for barrooms, red for whorehouses, and plain kerosene yellow to see where you were going. The lamps threw deep shadows across the street, which passing horsemen rode in and out of like cloud shadows out on the grass.

Then he reached Main. Main was a quieter street. Above the deputies' dead-line.

He thought he'd find a Chicago man at the bar-room of the Grand, at Turley's—the only Irishman to get permission to open a place on Main—or at Gus Grobard's. Gus put out a cold-cut spread, and had three horn players playing German music for dancing. It seemed to be the kind of place that a big city man would like.

No one at the Grand looked like the man Talbot had described. Turley had only card-games going, and some buyers at the bar.

He found George Peach at Grobard's, up on the bandstand, singing barbershop quartet with a gambler and two men who owned the eye-glass store on Fourth and Main. Lacy didn't know them, but he'd seen them through their show-window, fitting people out with eye-glasses.

The four of them made a good quartet; they sang well, and one of the horn players in the band was playing with them, making fancy toots around their singing. Peach had a corned-beef sandwich in his hand, and was waving it, keeping time as he sang. The room was crowded.

Lacy had known it was George Peach, when he stepped in through the swinging door. Peach was the first man anyone would have noticed in there.

He looked like a gentleman. And very young.

Peach was slim, and handsome, dressed in a fine cream summer suit with gray spats and black shoes, and he had a flat-crown straw on his head, pushed back enough so you could see he had his dark hair parted neatly in the middle, like a Yale-man swell. He was young and fresh-faced as a dandy pimp.

Lacy saw that he carried one revolver in a deep holster under his left arm. A .38, more than likely, and double-actioned the way most city men liked them. His fine suit had been cut to conceal the gun, and Lacy saw no other pistol on him; no knife, either.

He had a fine-featured face, and he smiled as he sang. A perfect young churchgoer, all in all, the apple of his mother's eye—if you didn't notice the revolver.

A devil with the girls, too, no doubt.

The Central Cattle Company must have spent a pretty penny to import this fine young fellow from Chicago. He was an import item, sure enough.

Lacy edged his way to the bar, asked for a glass of beer, and considered how best to kill this George Peach. The bar was very crowded and noisy, but he could hear the quartet starting another song. "*Come Into The Garden, Maude. . .*" They were singing this one, differently, softer.

Sliding down-hill. . . The song was softer, because George Peach wasn't singing with them anymore. He slid in beside Lacy at the bar, on his right, and smiled at him in

Gus Grobard's fine bar-mirror.

"Oh, dear," he said. "I startled you."

"You damn sure did," said Lacy, and he had.

Close up, George Peach didn't look as young, but he was still a handsome. Lacy looked into his eyes, and saw that Peach was a knowing man. Peach had gray-green eyes. He looked as though he'd seen the elephant. Between us, Lacy thought, we've seen it all.

Peach was close, standing on his right, where he could use his left hand to block Lacy's draw, and still get his own pistol free with his right.

There would be no taking him into the dark.

It would be here.

"Talbot?" Lacy said.

"Oh, yes, indeedy," George Peach said. "He came chasing into town to tell me all about it." He smiled. "Figured to be on the winning side, whichever, I suppose." He sighed. "Now, I put that damned sandwich down to come over here, and there's not even a plate of eggs on the bar and I'm starved."

He glanced at Lacy. "No need to fret over Mister Talbot, though. Some sad fellow took him out to the dump and shot him through the head. . ."

Lacy raised his left foot, and rested his boot-sole on the bar's brass rail.

"So," Peach said, and he leaned close to Lacy's right side, "you're the man who's been cracking the Company's hard cases. Well, I'm not surprised, not surprised at all. Talbot told me you were a fierce fellow, and you certainly look it. He described the scar; it's how I knew you. That, and your way of entering a room. . ."

Lacy took his right hand off his beer glass, and dropped it

to his side. Peach glanced down, and turned toward him, just a little bit. As he did that, Lacy reached down with his left hand, drew the Arkansas toothpick out of his left boot, and swung around and stabbed George Peach deep in the side.

Peach squalled and leaped back, fast as a cat. He'd been muscled hard, and the knife had gritted on a rib, slid in perhaps five inches, and stuck. When Peach leaped back, the knife was yanked out of Lacy's grip, still sticking out of the side of Peach's suit. The blood hadn't even started yet.

Lacy watched Peach in clear, quiet slowness. Peach was leaning back against the men behind him, the handle of the knife sticking out of his side. He reached inside his jacket and his hand came out again as quick as the needle of a sewing-machine, in-and-out. The pistol was nickel-plated .38. Behind him, men were just turning their heads to look at the trouble, just starting to open their mouths to remark on it, to complain. Peach's face looked like a madman's, contorted, gaping in rage, his teeth showing like an animal's. He and Lacy looked at each other through the slowness of everyone else. They were in a separate place.

Lacy drew and shot Peach in the belly.

They were close, and the flash and smoke billowed up between them and the bullet shoved Peach harder against the men behind him. The man from Chicago used that to hold himself up, he didn't take the time to grab for the edge of the bar. Lacy felt the pain before he saw the powder-flash. A sharp, sticking pain at the side of his neck, down near his shoulder. He shot Peach again, straight on, into his chest.

Then he heard men screaming, stomping, bucking away from the bar, trying to get away from the bullets. The sound came in on him. As they ran, as they herded away, they let George Peach fall. He fell slowly back, still making that animal's face at Lacy, aimed his bright pistol and fired again.

This one didn't hurt. It knocked Lacy's left leg out from under him and he fell to his knees by the bar, thumbed the hammer back on the Bisley and shot George Peach in the face.

Then Lacy heaved himself up, and hopped and shouldered his way through the yelling crowd. He had the revolver still in his hand, and they shouted and ran and shoved away from him as he limped. The noise and smells of the place were making him sick.

It was just too damned noisy. His left boot was too heavy for him. And he'd left the damned knife.

That was a fine knife, and he'd left it.

A man didn't get out of his way; he just stayed where he was and ducked down as if Lacy were still shooting. Lacy hit him as hard as he could with the Colt, and the man fell down.

Lacy felt sick to his stomach. He didn't know if he could get out out of there before he vomited all over the floor. He didn't want anyone to see that.

He didn't want anyone to see that, for sure.


Lacy limped down Second Street in the dark. He was limping hard; he couldn't feel anything in his left foot. It was like a block of wood.

Meager wouldn't have had a prayer in the world. Not a prayer in the world. Wonderful how fast Peach had gotten that .38 pistol out. And with a knife-blade sticking into his lung. Lacy thought how brave the men were that he fought. Bad men, but brave. . .

That second shot must have broken bones in his foot. He heard men shouting back up on Main Street. Likely the storeclerks would be coming after him; this would be his second killing in this town. One too many, for the storeclerks. . .

He'd get down to South Street, and wake Compton and get that buckskin vest from him. May as well have something to show beside a gray horse. . .

He thought some feeling might be coming back to his foot. It felt as though it was going to be hurting very bad. That Chicago son-of-a-bitch.


He rode into Angle Iron at dawn. He had his new fringed vest on, but everything else felt old as the hills. Compton had pulled his boot off in the back of the store, washed the foot and bandaged it. It had looked bad. The slug had gone clear through, but it had broken bones in there. Compton had managed to get Lacy's boot back on, and that had hurt like hell.

It still hurt like hell.

He'd said goodby to no-one at Miss Maynard's, except Big William, who'd seen him out back and helped him to saddle the gray.

"Say goodby to the girls for me. And Miss Maynard. Say goodby to Silky Perkins."

Big William had said he would, and had helped Lacy get up on the gray.

After that, it had been a long ride out. A long ride on a sunny morning. The gray rode smooth as a railroad train, but even so, Lacy's foot had hurt hard enough to put tears in his eyes. The other shot had drilled through the side of his neck, low down on the left, just under the skin.

That hurt, too. But not as bad as the foot. If it wasn't for that damn vigilance committee in town, he could have had a doctor for it. . . It was some temptation, it hurt so much, to go back to a doctor, and if the storeclerks wanted some fighting, well maybe he'd give it to them.

The sun was burning just over the horizon when he rode along the rise above the ranch. The day was coming into brightness. Most of the hands were out with the herd, but three men—looked like old Snell and a couple of others— were wrangling horses in the near corral. The other two were wrangling; Snell was sitting up on the rails, seemed to be putting a word in, now and then.

Lacy put the gray down the rise, and loped on past the calf corral, and past the horse wrangling. One man was bucking around, but Snell and the other man turned to watch him ride past. Snell waved, and Lacy raised a hand to him.

His hurt foot was pounding with the paces of the gray. It was going to be a chore, getting off and on.

When he cantered out into the yard, Lacy saw old man Meager, big as a statue, standing by the cookshack talking to Miss Louise. Smoke was rising from the stove-pipe behind them; One-eye Manuel cooking breakfast.

Lacy rode down to them.

They watched him come in, and when he pulled up, Meager glowered up at him and said, "Now, what the hell you do you mean, you pup—standing between another man and me?" The old man was gritting his teeth and looking fierce.

"I just figured you'd be too busy to bother with him," Lacy said. "Figured it was just a chore." He swung down off the gray as smoothly as he could.

"You're hurt," Miss Louise said. She came and touched his arm.

"I turned my ankle in the fight," Lacy said. "Nothing more than that." No use staying here. No use tempting the Company to make it a personal matter. To send another man out.

"Come into the house," she said.

"Thank you, no. I'll be riding on, now."

She turned pale, and looked plainer than ever, her brown eyes big in that long horse's face.

"What happened in that fight, boy?" old Meager said.

"The man is dead. I doubt they'll try with another. They've made considerable noise out here already." Lacy leaned against the gray, took some weight off that foot. "If I'm not here, they'll have no personal grudge. . ."

Old Meager gave him a look.

"You folks have your horses, now. Go on and hire four or five tough young buckaroos. I think the Company'll call it quits. And now, you folks know about the railroad's coming through."

"Mister Talbot's run away, I believe," Meager said, looking as if he'd like to get his one hand on him.

"Not far enough or fast enough. The Company man killed him." Lacy was feeling sick to his stomach, he was so tired. It was time to be going. . . "I came for my saddle. . . my war-bag."

"I'll get them for you, boy," old Meager said, and he lead the gray away, muttering and shaking his white-maned head.

Miss Louise kept her hand on Lacy's arm.

"Stay a while with us," she said. "Stay and rest." She was watching him in a sad and gentle way.

"No," he said. "I'd better be riding."

"If," she said. "If I were a. . .a pretty woman. Then—?"

"You're not pretty at all, Louise, but you're a beautiful woman, just the same and more than most men ever deserve." And that was certainly true.

He could stay. . . he could surely stay. Lacy had the strange feeling of imagining their children—his and Louise's. It was such a clear thing it was almost real—as if it

237

were *certain*. They would have two boys. Two big, ugly, sweet-natured boys. And damned if he could say how he knew it.

But the Company would be after him. He'd done too much against them. They'd be wanting to find out all there was to find out about Finn Lacy. And someday, they'd know.

No settling down on Angle Iron. No plain-faced, loving, long-legged wife. No boys to raise hell and hold the land.

None of that.

A dandy young killer—a fine young pimp and sharper—a terrible fast gun named Buckskin Frank Leslie, had robbed him of that.

Old Meager came leading the gray. He'd put Lacy's saddle on him, and strapped the roll and war-bag to the cantle. The Sharps was in the saddle-boot.

"Damn it, boy," the old man said, and he looked hard at Louise. "Damn it! What are you cutting out for?"

"Time to go, sir."

"Why? We'll hire on men, now. We'll fight anything they try. No man will lay a hand on you!" He put his huge, gnarled paw on the handle of the Walker Colt. "Stay with us, son. Make a home here." He glanced at Louise and flushed pink. "We want you to stay. . ."

Louise smiled at the old man. "No, Mister Meager, he has to go." She looked at Lacy. "Isn't that so?"

"Yes, my dear," Lacy said. "Otherwise, I'd stay forever. . ." He limped to her and kissed her lightly on the lips, then he went to the gray and mounted it.

He rode up out of the yard, and he didn't look back. He didn't look back until he reached the rise. His leg was on fire with the wound, and he was glad about that pain—it kept a worse one from him.

It was coming to be a perfect morning, bright and cool.

He saw two larks swinging together in the air to the south, high over the endless grass.

At the ridge of the rise, he pulled the gray in, and looked back. Far below, the two figures stood still in the ranch-yard. Watching him.

The old man raised his arm to wave at him. The woman stood still.

Lacy turned the gray's head, spurred him, and rode away.